Piece of music
the culeer

D1800126

INSECURITY
and a
BOTTLE of
MERLOT

LIKE SISTERS, BOOK TWO

BRIA MARCHE

Copyright © 2014
All Rights Reserved

AUTHOR'S NOTE

This book is a work of fiction by Bria Marche. Names, characters, places and incidents are products of the author's imagination or are used solely for entertainment. Any resemblance to actual events or persons, living or dead, is entirely coincidental.

The scanning, uploading and distribution of this book via the Internet or any other means without the permission of the publisher is illegal and punishable by law. Please purchase only authorized electronic editions, and do not participate in or encourage electronic piracy of copyrighted materials. Your support of the author's rights is appreciated.

ABOUT THE AUTHOR

Bria Marche is a contemporary romance writer. Though originally from San Jose, California, she has lived in the Midwest region of the United States for quite some time. She is a member of numerous writers' organizations, including Fiction for All, Fiction Factor, and Writers-Online.

Other than writing, she enjoys all forms of art. She especially likes creating outdoor garden projects, designing and painting gourd birdhouses, and making handmade soaps. She is an avid gardener and a world traveler—which includes hot-air ballooning across Italy—and loves birdwatching, hiking, and bicycling.

Book three in *Like Sisters* series is available now at:
http://briamarche.com/books/

Be the first to be notified of new releases at:
http://briamarche.com/newsletter/

Visit my website at:
http://briamarche.com/

Chapter One

He sat in the car, fidgeting as he watched, even though he was well hidden by the shade of the ancient oak trees along the curb. His vantage point was perfect. The house was only half a block ahead on the left. Completely out of his element, he waited. It was so beneath him, but he was angry and had to seek revenge against her somehow. She'd ruined his career and life. Everything he ever wanted was at his fingertips just a few nights ago, but now? He had nothing, not even a place to live. In an instant of public, brutal humiliation, she'd snatched it all away. *She'll pay, the bitch. They're all going to pay.*

She walked out the front door with Reggie at eight o'clock sharp.

Must be morning walk time. Jack peered through the binoculars. He didn't see a set of keys in Mia's hand. Maybe he'd get lucky after all. He waited for them to turn the corner then exited his car and cautiously approached the house. *Why am I worried? The neighbors don't even know what happened.* He turned the knob, hoping the front door was unlocked. It swung open. Jack smiled. He didn't have the luxury of time, so he went directly to the spot where her keys always hung. There they were, on the rack in the foyer. Her purse sat on the bench below as it had every day that he'd lived there. Mia was a creature of habit—that he was certain of. A single key hung next to the set Mia used daily. He compared it to the new house key on her ring. It matched perfectly. He tried it in the front door, and the lock turned. *Good. It's the spare house key and it's going with me. Thanks, Mia, for being so predictable and making this like taking candy from a baby.*

The absence of his belongings was noticeable as he did a walk-through of the house. All of his possessions had been transferred to his brother's house. Mick hadn't sounded too pleased about the moving company leaving a message Monday morning, wanting to know when they could bring over Jack's belongings. Jack hadn't told his brother about the breakup before that point, being too preoccupied with finding a way to get revenge on her. His wife. The bitch.

"Hey Mick, it's Jack. Sorry about the movers. I'll take care of it. That was Mia's doing. I need to talk to you, Bro. Give me a call when you get off work. I'm not moving back to New Rochelle, but I may have to camp out with you for a few weeks if that's okay. I'll start looking for a place to live in the city right away. It will make job hunting much easier. Anyway, like I said, give me a call, and I'll take you out to dinner and explain everything. Thanks, Bro. See ya."

Jack had to do a lot of explaining. He wasn't

particularly close to Mick—Jack didn't make time for family or friendships and hadn't seen his brother in over a year even though they lived less than thirty miles apart. He was only interested in climbing the corporate ladder. He'd been going places in a hurry until Mia threw a wrench into everything. Now, he had to grovel for a place to stay, and he knew that Mick wasn't fooled by his facade of caring.

***

The heavy weight that had rested on Mia's shoulders for nearly three years was gone. No more anxiety, no more drama, no more Jack. *I wasted three years of my life with that jerk. I can start fresh with a new focus. I know exactly what I want,* she thought as she walked her beloved dog, Reggie.

Aaron Daniels was Mia's new focus and vice versa. He'd loved her for years, and Mia had finally realized he was indeed the right one. He always had been. She'd just needed a two-timing jerk of a husband to make it crystal clear. Jack was out, and Aaron was in.

"C'mon Reggie, let's go home."

Mia had a full day planned already. It included shopping with Vic, Tina, Karen, and Sasha in the city until three and, at five thirty, taking a fiftieth wedding anniversary portrait, which would be placed in the *Tarrytown Daily Voice*. She'd stop by Aaron's house later. Mia wasn't sure if being public with Aaron this soon was appropriate—Tarrytown was a small village, and people would talk. A private dinner at his house would be a smarter choice for the time being.

Mia returned home, showered, and dressed. Today, she would take time to blow dry her hair and style it nicely. Dress shopping would be fun. Vic needed something snazzy for her cousin's wedding next weekend. Of course, Vic's real objective was to look hot for the man on her arm at that event, who would be none other than *the* sexy Max Cole—a guy like Max needed *the* in front of his name. Max, according to Vic, was the hottest, sexiest hunk of manflesh she'd ever laid eyes on. With Mia's blessing, Vic had invited Max to join her at the wedding, and now Vic was on a mission to find the dress of the century.

Mia met the girls at the train station. They planned to shop at Saks, Bergdorf Goodman, and Bloomingdale's. There wasn't time to go anywhere else, but Vic was sure to find what she wanted in one of those stores.

Vic took her time describing Max Cole to her captive audience during the train ride into the city. "You guys, he is the hottest thing next to the sun—I swear to you. You have to meet him before we leave for the wedding. All of you be at my house Saturday at eleven sharp. I'll act like you were helping me get ready. That way you can see what I'm talking about. Just keep your hands off, or honest to God, I'll kill you all."

Mia laughed at Vic's enthusiasm. "I can't make it, but tell Max hi for me, okay?"

"What the hell does that mean?" Tina asked. "Aren't you curious to see what he looks like?"

"Mia is friends with Max already," Vic piped in.

Three heads spun like tops toward Mia.

"Jeez, Vic—thanks."

"Oops, sorry, Chica—my bad."

"Okay, spill," Karen said. "How do you explain meeting this guy before the rest of us?"

"Mia knew Max before I did," Vic said as Mia shot the shit eye at her again. "Just tell them how you became friends so I can stop putting my foot in my mouth," Vic said, exasperated.

"Oh, for crap's sake, Vic, since you have diarrhea of the mouth, I'll tell them. Max is the wilderness guide for the Boy Scouts' yearly outing at Putnam Valley. He's the one who drove my car home for me after I sprained my ankle."

"And Vic met up with you when you got back to Tarrytown? Didn't you get home on a Thursday while we were at work?" Tina asked suspiciously.

"No, you goof," Vic said. "I met Max last week. Obviously, I made quite an impression on him since he agreed to go to the wedding with me."

"So, what am I missing here?" Tina asked. "Your time lines don't jibe."

"Okay, I'm only telling you this so we can get off the subject. Max stopped by my house last week unexpectedly to see how my ankle was. That's when Vic met him. She was instantly and shamelessly smitten and asked him to go to lunch with her. The rest is her story since I wasn't there."

"I can meet him too, right? Am I invited to your house, Vic?" Sasha asked.

"Yes, you can come, too. The train's slowing down. Let's go—we have some serious shopping to do."

***

They struck out at Saks and Bergdorf Goodman, so after lunch, they headed to Bloomingdale's. There, in the window, in Vic's face, was the dress of the century. She gasped, let out a high-pitched squeak, and ran like a track star for the entrance. "It's here—it's here," she yelled back at the girls, then disappeared into the massive store with the rest of them trying to keep up. Vic didn't care about impressing anyone but Max. She couldn't believe her good fortune in having *the* Max Cole for an entire day and into the reception at night. *I wonder if he can dance. He's got to be a beer kind of guy. Wine doesn't seem like something he'd drink. Too foo-foo for him.* Vic wanted to be the perfect date. Nothing was going to surprise her. She intended to make Saturday the best night of her life.

Chapter Two

The kitchen buzzed with activity. Mia arrived at Aaron's house at seven with Reggie in tow. Aaron had given her a set of his house keys, just because. With any luck, Mia's house would go on the market soon, and she and Reggie could move in with Aaron. This would be the house she'd call home. She'd always loved Aaron's house, which was in the most beautiful and historic neighborhood of Tarrytown. Her dreams were coming true. They would make this place not only a beautiful, cozy house but also a home filled with love and happiness. In a few years, after she and Aaron married, there would be kids running around. Mia smiled as she daydreamed.

She tossed the salad and set the table on the patio. The grill, already fired up, waited for Aaron's expertise. He proudly acknowledged the fact that he made the best barbecue chicken in Westchester County. The secret was his mother's sauce recipe. Only the Daniels family was privy to the special ingredient. Sometime soon, Mia would be told.

"Hey, beat it," he said, laughing, as Mia peered over his

shoulder at the stove to see what ingredients he was stirring together. "Isn't there something you need to do, like sit down and enjoy a glass of Merlot?"

"Okay, but someday, mister, I'll find out what that secret ingredient is. First, you get a kiss, and then I'll sit."

"You know what that means, don't you? You need to be one of the clan before we can share something that well-guarded with you," Aaron teased.

"When the time comes, that better not be your proposal." Mia poured each of them a glass of wine and sat at the table.

"So, what's going on with Jack? Have you heard from him?"

"Only the messages and texts he sent me after the ordeal last Friday night. He was really pissed off, Aaron, almost to the point of sounding scary in the one text I read."

"So, you didn't listen to or read everything he sent?"

"No. I was so relieved the night was over, and I didn't want to hear his ranting. I read one text and deleted everything else."

"Did you call a divorce attorney yet?" Aaron stirred the sauce on the stove. Concern for Mia furrowed his brows.

"I called on Monday and met with him this morning. He drew up the papers for me and sent copies to Jack's brother's house. That's the only address I've got. I might be wrong, but I assume that's where Jack is staying. I'm glad I found an attorney right here in town. Everything should go faster with a local attorney than one in the city.

Oh, and by the way, I want to give you my spare key. I'm not going to leave one outside anymore. Jack knew where my hiding places were."

"Good idea, sweetheart. Better safe than sorry. I'll be happy when all of this negative stuff is behind you and we can tell everyone we're a couple."

"Me too. I love you *and* your barbecue chicken. Let's eat already. My stomach is growling."

***

Vic tossed and turned all night from excitement. *Damn it—I need to sleep! I can't go to this wedding tomorrow with bags under my eyes.* She barely dozed then finally got up at seven thirty, irritated by lack of sleep. She had a big day to get ready for. A strong pot of coffee brewed while she wrapped the wedding gift for her cousin. *Who wouldn't want a back massager?* She finished the box off with a large silver bow. At eight thirty she called Tina. "Hey, girl, why don't you and Sasha come over now? I'm going to need help with my hair and nails anyway, plus I'll make breakfast. How about it—*pleeease?*"

"Sure, we'll be over at nine. Out."

Vic was resting on the couch with a pillow under her head and cucumber slices over her eyelids when someone banged on the door. "It's open if you're Tina and Sasha. Otherwise stay out," she yelled from the couch.

The door opened, and Sasha walked in with Tina right behind her, carrying a satchel of hair products and makeup. "Check out Vic," Sasha said, laughing. "That actually works. Models do it all the time when they party too late."

Vic got up and welcomed her friends into the kitchen. "What do you guys want for breakfast?"

"I'll have dry toast," Sasha responded.

"The hell you will. Not in my house, chicky mama. We're having pancakes with a lot of butter and maple syrup." She smacked her butt. "I didn't get this big ass from eating dry toast."

"Fine," Sasha said. "I'll have one pancake. Can I help you cook?"

"Of course. Get over here. Have you ever been in a kitchen before?"

"Yes, smarty pants. Oh, and guess what? Somebody put an offer in on my apartment. How exciting, right?"

"That's awesome, babe. It'll be a riot helping you house hunt. Then, of course, we'll hold a huge house-warming party. Better start stocking up on the wine," Vic said, winking at her new friend. Her phone rang as she was flipping the pancakes. "Take over, Sasha. I gotta see who wants me."

"I'm afraid," Sasha whined, almost in a panic.

"Let me do it," Tina said. "Remind me to teach you how to cook when we get home."

"Thanks, Tina."

"Hey, Vic, how's it going?" Max asked at the other end of the line.

"I'm awesome, of course." She laughed.

"Yeah, I know you are. I have a slight problem."

I bet his pants zipper is stuck, and he needs my assistance. I could only wish. "That's impossible, Max. You're perfect."

Max laughed, and she was glad he appreciated her sense of humor. "Anyway, here's the deal. I have my Harley, which you've seen, and a pickup. Not the best options for taking a beautiful woman, such as yourself, to a wedding. Would it be too gauche if we took your car today? I'll end up with dead bugs on my clothes and teeth if I show up on my Harley. I'd love to take you out on my bike some other time though."

"So, we're going out again? Is that what you're saying, Mr. Cole?" she asked coquettishly.

Max laughed again. "Only if you want to, babe."

"Of course I want to," she replied with a fist pump.

"Cool, then. I'll see you at twelve thirty. Bye, hot stuff."

"Bye, Max." Vic hung up and danced around the kitchen while her friends laughed.

"Excited a little?" Tina teased.

"Oh yeah... oh yeah... oh yeah. You'll understand when you see Max Adonis. I guaran-damn-tee it."

The doorbell rang. "It has to be Karen," they chimed in together as Sasha ran to the door.

***

That's strange. Mia stood in the foyer, staring at the key rack. *Where in the hell is my spare key? There's no other place I would have put it. I'm positive it was hanging here.* She felt goose bumps forming on her arms even though the temperature indoors was perfectly comfortable. She searched her purse, the house, her car. The spare key was nowhere to be found. *I'm not going crazy. It was here—I'm sure of it.* She continued searching for another thirty minutes before giving up.

She called Aaron at the camera store. "Hi, honey, it's me."

"I hope so. I wouldn't expect anyone else to call me honey," Aaron joked. When she didn't answer, he said, "Mia? Is everything okay?"

"I know the answer to this, but I'll ask anyway: did I already give you my spare house key?"

"No, you didn't."

"That's what I was afraid of. It's missing."

"How is that possible? You just changed the locks a week ago, and you never misplace anything."

"Yeah," she said, "and that's what has me rattled. I had the new key fitted for every door in the house. I haven't put the spare outside, not once, since they changed the locks. It's been hanging on the key rack in the foyer since last Saturday. Now, it's gone."

"Do you think one of the movers took it when they packed up Jack's things?"

"I bet you're right, but why? Those guys don't know me from Adam. Why would they want my house key?"

"To steal things, honey. You're going to have to change the locks again, and the sooner the better. You can't risk it—not living alone like you do. Reggie is a good watch dog, but what if you aren't home, and someone sneaks in?"

"You're right, damn it. That cost me three hundred bucks. I'll call the locksmith again. I hope they can just rekey the locks. Okay, I'll let you get back to work. Thanks, honey."

"Come over for dinner, Mia. Sounds like you're a little stressed. I'll be home by five thirty."

Chapter Three

Tina worked on Vic's unruly hair, comb in hand and a dozen bobby pins pinched between her lips. Sasha painted her nails, wearing her lime-green, cat-eyed readers so she wouldn't make any mistakes. The coral-colored polish would look great with Vic's olive skin and raven hair.

"Am I'm doing a good job?" Sasha asked.

"Sure, hon, just make sure to keep the polish off my cuticles."

"Maybe I can work at the salon doing mani-pedi's," Sasha suggested enthusiastically.

"*Yeah… no.* Are you deranged, Sasha? You make more money in one hour of modeling than you would in a month of polishing someone's nails. Anyway, Mia is going to start taking pictures of you for your portfolio and our advertising. Make sure your little fanny is at the salon on Tuesday so we can get started."

"Okay. That sounds exciting. When can we start house hunting?"

"We'll get together next weekend and start looking."

"Cool. You guys know the best areas to live in even

though Tarrytown isn't very big."

"That's right—leave it to us. We won't steer you wrong." Vic glanced at the clock—11:58 a.m. "Are you guys almost done? I have a dress to put on."

"Yep," Tina said. "Go ahead and get dressed—we're finished."

Vic left for the bedroom. "No peeking. Wait until I come out."

Tina, Karen, and Sasha waited in the kitchen for Vic's grand entrance. They gossiped while enjoying a fresh pot of coffee and cookies Karen had found in the pantry. The clip-clop of Vic's heels sounded on the glistening hardwood floors as she neared the kitchen. They spun their chairs around to face her as she entered.

"Holy shit, Vic, are you hot or what?" Tina squealed. She let out a long wolf whistle while Karen and Sasha gasped with their mouths gaping open.

"Do you really think I'm hot? Is my ass too big?" Vic asked, knowing the answer to both questions already.

"You look amazing. You're even hotter than me," Sasha said.

Vic pranced around the room, pleading with Sasha to show her how to strut like a model on a catwalk. The girls were enjoying the moment when the doorbell rang.

"Shit—he's here!" Vic yelped.

"Yeah," Karen said. "He's supposed to be, dummy. You should be happy he's on time. Points for Max." They all gathered on the couch to watch him enter. "I wish I had a bag of popcorn."

Vic took a deep breath and opened the front door. Max stood on the porch with a grin that almost reached his ears. He gave his own version of a wolf whistle as he looked her up and down. "Somebody get me the smelling salts before I pass out. What a beauty. Good God, I'm going to be the envy of everyone today."

"Oh, stop it," Vic said although she looked as if she were loving every word. "Come in already, and meet my friends. Max, this is Karen, Tina, and Sasha—my girls."

"Hi, Max. We've heard so much about you. Vic can't stop raving," Tina said just to embarrass Vic.

The three of them looked Max up and down, appreciating everything they saw. "Wow... Vic wasn't kidding," Sasha said. "You're hot."

"Sasha, jeez, can you please zip it?"

"Sorry. Nice to meet you."

"Well, it's nice to meet you too. I'm sure we'll all be close friends soon," Max said. "What, no Mia?"

"Not today. Should we head out? You can drive my car while I call out the directions. Lock up, girls. See you later." Vic looked back, grinned, and blew air kisses to her friends.

"Wow, not bad... not bad at all." Tina downed her cup of cold coffee. "Wanna go out to lunch? Karen, call Mia and see if she wants to meet us at Morey's."

***

A late lunch at Morey's was just what they needed. Mia had to run her key issue by the girls, and of course, they had to ooh and aah about Max. Mia sat at a bar table, waiting for everyone to show up. She ordered two bottles of Merlot because she knew that was what they'd be drinking. She poured four glasses. The girls arrived and air kissed her when they reached the table.

"Why didn't you come over to Vic's house this morning?" Sasha asked. "That Max is way too gorgeous."

Mia laughed. "You're preaching to the choir, sister."

"What does that mean?"

"Never mind, sit down. I have something to run by you guys. It's kind of scary, but I want everyone's individual opinion of what I should do."

All eyes were on Mia, wineglasses suspended in midair.

"What?" Tina asked.

"Okay. So, I changed all of my locks last Saturday morning, right?"

"Yes," they agreed.

"What I didn't tell any of you was that Jack texted me and called about eighty-five thousand times Friday night after the ordeal at the promotion party."

"He did that to me, too," Sasha said, sounding worried.

"Same here." Karen looked at each one of them.

"Well, shit! Why didn't we tell each other?" Mia asked. "He actually threatened me in one text. Everything else I deleted without reading or listening to. I didn't want to focus on Jack or even hear his voice again. Now, my extra house key is missing. I'm positive I hung it in the foyer on the rack. I was going to give it to Aaron instead of hiding it outside, so I went to grab it this morning, but it was gone."

"I wonder if Jack had anything to do with it. So, now what?" Tina asked.

"I'm not sure. Aaron thought it might be the movers that loaded Jack's stuff in the truck. I guess that makes sense. They were in the house after all. I thought for a minute that it might be Jack, but how would he have gotten in? Aaron's theory makes more sense. I guess I'll have the locksmith rekey the locks."

"Or catch the thief in his tracks," Tina suggested.

"How am I going to do that without risking my own safety?"

Karen said, "Just hide a spy cam outside. They'll never get their foot in the door because you have deadbolts and chain locks anyway. Why spend more money rekeying the locks? We can catch the person on camera and have their butt arrested. You can download the video footage right to your phone. You don't even need to be home to catch them."

"That sounds too scary to me. I'll just call the locksmith. Let's move on to something else... I wonder how Vic and Max will hit if off after spending an entire day together."

"I don't know, but man, would I love to be in her shoes." Tina was almost drooling.

"You said it, sister. Max Cole is one hot hunk of manflesh," Karen agreed.

"Did anyone take a picture of them together before they left?"

"I did," Sasha said triumphantly. Apparently, she'd been the only one with enough brain cells left, after staring at Max, to snap a picture of them together.

"Well, let's see it." The girls crowded around Sasha's cell phone and hyperventilated over the picture. Max and Vic looked as though they'd just stepped off a *Vogue* magazine cover. Mia's heart did a little flutter as she looked at the snapshot. *What the hell was that? There's no way I'm going to let myself become jealous of Max and Vic. No way in hell.*

***

Vic directed Max to the Pelham Bay Golf Course in the Bronx. The manicured gardens and lawns made a beautiful setting for the outdoor wedding planned that day. The afternoon was sunny and eighty-two degrees.

"Just a heads-up, Max—my family is pretty crazy. There are a lot of us, being Puerto Rican and all. Plus we like to let loose and have fun. You do like to dance, don't you?"

"I haven't danced since I went to my junior prom in high school," he said, looking at her with his sexy grin. "But I'm not going to have a choice, am I?"

"You got that right, mister. There's no way someone as hot as you is going to sit in a corner and go unnoticed. I'm getting you out there, baby, and we're gonna shake up the dance floor. We'll have a great time. My family is a riot. I need to figure out how to keep all my cousins off you though. There's going to be a lot of hot, young chicas there that would love your attention."

"Are you worried?" he asked with a chuckle.

"Nah... I can take all of them. They know better than to mess with me. I'll whip their asses."

"My eyes are focused only on you. You look stunning today, Vic."

"Thanks, Max. You're not so bad yourself."

The wedding ceremony was glorious. The bride, Vic's cousin Serena Lopez, wore a dress that could rival anything in a royal wedding. Serena's beautiful, single sister, Olivia, was the maid of honor, and the groom's brother Élan was the Best Man. Ten couples, miniature bride, flower girl, and ring bearer made their way down the rose-petal-lined path while the guests snapped picture after picture.

***

Max watched as tears of joy wet Vic's cheeks. Her smile illuminated her entire face. He smiled, too, and squeezed her hand. *She's a spitfire, all right, but sweet and sentimental. I like this girl.*

Vic caught the bouquet, and Max caught the garter.

"You know what this means, right, Max?" she taunted. "You have to slow dance with me now, just us, in front of the whole world. Don't worry—it's only for a few minutes, then everyone else will join in. But for those few minutes, you're all mine. I'll take it easy on you, babe—I promise." She laughed and gave him a peck on the cheek.

They danced in front of the crowd of onlookers while

the smoke machine set the mood, and the spotlight was fixated on them. The music played slow and sexy. Hoots and hollers came from everyone watching because they looked that good together. Vic nuzzled in close with her arms wrapped around Max's neck. He pulled her in even tighter.

"Max Cole, I think you're enjoying this," she whispered in his ear.

"Victoria Alonso, I'm enjoying you."

The bride and groom made their exit at eleven o'clock, and the party began to wind down. "What do you think, Vic? You wanna blow this pop stand?"

"Sure. Let's go to my house. We can have a drink there. What's your pleasure?" she asked, her voice sultry.

"Seriously?"

"Seriously... beer or wine?"

"I'm a beer kind of guy, but you knew that. There's time... plenty of time to get better acquainted. Now, let's go have that beer, gorgeous."

Chapter Four

Mia called the locksmith Sunday morning, hoping to leave a message. A recorded voice said the office would be closed until August 4. *Well, what the heck?* She felt anxious and irritated.

"C'mon, Reggie, let's go for a walk." She grabbed the leash and snapped it to Reggie's collar. She pulled the front door closed out of habit, then turned back and went inside to grab her keys, slipping them into her pocket. Mia exited again, giving the doorknob a twist to make sure it was locked. Going through the daily process of walking Reggie made Mia stop and take note of her actions. *Crap! I never lock the front door when I walk Reggie. I never gave it any thought until the extra key went missing. Anybody could have come in and taken the key, even Jack.* She scanned up and down the street, looking for that familiar white BMW. Nothing. Goose bumps rose on her arms. *Okay, Mia, stop freaking yourself out. I'll keep the deadbolt and chain lock secured when I'm inside. And in a week, I'll get the locks rekeyed.* She turned the corner with Reggie.

***

The man wearing the baseball cap and sunglasses waited an extra minute then nonchalantly went up the sidewalk, unlocked the front door, and slipped inside. He headed straight for the basement. He knew Mia rarely went down there. "Out of sight, out of mind," she always said. Truth be told, Mia didn't use the basement for anything except storage because it creeped her out. It was the perfect way for Jack to come and go at will.

He descended the twelve steps and pulled the string on the ceiling light. The windows were large enough to easily fit through. *This will work out fine. It doesn't hurt to have another way of getting in, just in case Mia changes the locks again.* Jack unlatched all the basement windows then went back upstairs. Just to mess with her, he pulled one of the kitchen chairs out about a foot from the table. "That will drive her nuts." He peered out the windows to make sure nobody was outside, then left.

***

The neighborhood walk ended, and Mia returned home with Reggie. She had lunch plans with Aaron and wanted to look especially nice for him. She felt good about their relationship and where it was going. *Soon, we'll take it to the next level.* Mia wanted to be intimate with Aaron. She was ready and dreamed about it when she lay in bed at night. Aaron would wait for her to initiate sex, being the gentleman he was.

This whole thing with Jack had Mia unnerved. She hadn't heard from him at all since the initial flood of messages. That didn't sit well with her. Jack had always been a loose cannon, and his silence worried her more than anything else. Unfortunately, her thoughts were more on Jack and the divorce than on Aaron, the man she loved. She couldn't wait until it was over and Jack was nothing more than a bad memory. Mia hoped to hear from her attorney that Jack had signed the papers.

Reggie bolted for the kitchen after Mia took off his leash. She laughed as he plopped down on the cool tile floor. His tongue tapped the floor as he panted. "Need some water, Reg?" She grabbed his water bowl and emptied the tepid water into the sink then filled it with clean, cold water and turned to set it on the mat. She watched, as if in slow motion, as the bowl fell to the floor, spilling water everywhere. Reggie yelped and ran for the bedroom.

"Son of a bitch—I know that chair wasn't pulled out when I left!" Mia's hand shook as she made the call to Aaron.

"Hi, sweetheart, what's up?"

"Can you please come over? I need you right now."

"Mia, what's wrong? Are you okay?"

"No, I'm not. I'm seriously going crazy. Please come over now."

"I'll be there in ten minutes. Hang tight, honey."

Mia sat on the porch, waiting. She fidgeted, unable to control the trembling of her hands. Aaron's car rounded the corner and squealed to a stop in her driveway. He rushed up the sidewalk and embraced her.

"Sweetheart, what happened?"

Mia began sobbing with her head in her hands. "Aaron, somebody came into the house. I mean just this morning, a half hour ago."

"What? Are you okay? How do you know? That's it—I'm calling the cops."

"Wait. Just hold me for a minute. We need to figure this out." She wiped her eyes.

"Do you want to go to my house?"

"We've got to go inside. I didn't look around yet. I ran out when I saw it."

"When you saw what?"

"Come with me. I'll show you." Mia took Aaron by the hand and led him into the kitchen. "Be careful—the floor is wet. There." She pointed to the chair.

"I don't understand what you're pointing at."

"The chair. When I took Reggie for our morning walk, all of the chairs were pushed in. I had my coffee and toast at the breakfast bar this morning. I never sat at the table. I locked the front door when we left, and we were gone for about thirty minutes. This is how the chair was when we got back. I haven't touched anything."

"Stay in the kitchen, honey. I'm going to search the house thoroughly." He opened the door to the garage and flipped on the light to check there first. "Come, Reggie—you can help me."

He searched the entire house and then returned to the

kitchen. "Everything looks normal, sweetheart. None of the doors or windows appear to have been tampered with."

"There's still the basement. I hardly ever go down there. It's dark and creepy."

"Okay, I'll be right back. Stay put." Aaron grabbed a flashlight, then he and Reggie disappeared down the flight of stairs. Mia heard each descending step and counted them in her head. She knew he'd reached the bottom when she heard him pull the strings on the individual ceiling lights. A few minutes later, he and Reggie came back upstairs.

"Mia, when was the last time you were down there?"

"Last year, when I brought up the Christmas decorations. Why?"

"Every window latch was open, and the dust on the sills was disturbed. I locked them again. My question is, if it's truly a thief, wouldn't they have taken something?"

"It's Jack."

"What?"

"It's him. He's messing with me. He wants to drive me crazy. I have to warn Karen and Sasha. He left them threatening messages, too. We have to get restraining orders right away."

"Honey, he's still your husband and he hasn't done anything to warrant a restraining order against him."

"I told him I changed the locks and not to come back. That means if he does have the key, he trespassed to get it. He stole it."

"That's a good point. We need to catch him in the act

so you can press charges against him. It's probably the only thing that will stick. Let's go buy a camera to hide in the bushes."

"Tina and Karen were right. They told me to do that yesterday."

"So, you thought it was Jack all along?"

"In my gut I did. I'm sorry I didn't tell you. You've put up with my Jack bs for way too long."

"Here's the plan, Mia. We're going to set him up. We'll get the camera, and if he is watching when you take Reggie out, he'll make his move then. I don't think Jack is dangerous. I'm guessing he's only trying to unnerve you. Anyway, we'll catch him on video in the act of trespassing. That should be reason enough to get a restraining order against him. Until this is taken care of, I'm staying here with you. I'll keep my car in the garage, so he won't see it. I'll protect you no matter what."

She wrapped her arms around Aaron's neck and cried. "I appreciate you so much. I wish we'd started our lives together years ago."

"Shhh... honey. We have each other now, and that's what counts. Nobody is ever going to ruin that for us, especially Jack. Now, let's go buy that camera."

***

Jack had been staying at his brother's house for a week, which irritated Mick to no end. They weren't close, and he knew Jack was nothing but a user. He gave Jack a month to figure something out, then he would have to go.

They put Jack's belongings in storage. Mick wasn't about to let his brother unpack and get too comfortable.

"So, tell me," Mick asked over dinner, "how did you lose your job? Weren't you in a top position at Plan-It Kidz?"

"Mia caused this entire mess. She was jealous of my advancing career and fabricated an enormous, slanderous story about me to my bosses. She wanted me out of her life and house. Losing my job was the perfect reason to kick me out. Plus she was cheating on me... the bitch."

"That doesn't sound like Mia."

"Well, it's been some time since you saw her. I've wanted to come by and visit you a number of times, but she always had an excuse why we couldn't. She's changed since we got married—for the worse. To be honest with you, I'm glad we split up. She's become paranoid and neurotic lately."

"That's really weird. So, have you started looking for work?"

"Yeah, I have feelers out everywhere. As a matter of fact, I have an interview at Saks next week. They're looking for a buyer in their men's-clothing department. It's a great opportunity. I should be able to advance quickly with my credentials."

"That sounds good. I hope it works out for you."

"No problem, brother. It's in the bag."

Chapter Five

Aaron and Mia snuggled on the couch together and watched TV Sunday night. Reggie lay on the floor, content. They'd purchased the camera earlier and installed it in the shrubs just outside the front door. Now, the waiting game would begin, and they'd see if anyone showed up.

"Aaron, something as simple and normal as watching TV together means the world to me."

"I'm sorry things with Jack didn't turn out the way you hoped they would, honey. I want to give you a happy life. We'll get married soon and raise a family together."

"I want that too," Mia said, as she turned the TV off. "Let's go to bed."

A surprised look crossed Aaron's face. It was only nine o'clock. "Okay. Where do you want me to sleep?"

She smiled and took him by the hand to the master bedroom. "I want you to sleep with me... for the rest of my life." Mia folded back the bedspread and dimmed the lights, creating a soft, glowing ambiance. She turned on the radio and set it to a blues station with the volume low.

"I want you, Aaron Daniels, right now."

"Mia, I love you so much. I've dreamed of this day for years, and now my dreams are coming true."

Mia lifted her arms as Aaron slowly raised the tank top over her head. He unbuttoned her white shorts and slid them down her tanned legs. Mia unzipped Aaron's jeans, releasing the growing shaft that he no longer had control of. He lifted her, and she wrapped her legs around his hips, feeling his rock-hard manhood against her body. They gave deep moans from their pent-up need for each other. The passion escalated as he carried her to the bed. He pulled his T-shirt over his head and dropped his jeans to the floor. Aaron straddled Mia, leaning down to kiss her. She ached for his touch. She couldn't have stopped the quivering that took over her body even if she'd wanted to. The way Aaron licked and kissed her most private parts felt magical. She couldn't believe what this man was doing to her. "Aaron, it was you all along. You've always been the man for me. Make love to me, and don't ever stop."

"I can't believe how you make me feel, Mia." He moaned as he entered her.

She gasped as she pulled him in deeper, thrusting her hips upward to meet his every stroke.

"We have to slow down, honey," he said. "I can't last much longer. You have me on the edge."

"Just take me. I can't slow down either. I need everything you have right now. I'm going to explode."

They climaxed together in a frenzy of lust and love. Neither of them had ever experienced such intense passion before. The sweat glistened on their bodies as they lay, spent, in each other's arms.

"I love you, honey, and can't wait to make you my wife."

She smiled and kissed him, tasting the sweat that beaded on his upper lip. She licked it off and kissed him again. "I never knew it before, but you're all I've ever wanted." She fell asleep in his arms.

***

Mia called the girls to set up a Tuesday lunch date. She needed to tell them to be careful. She didn't have evidence yet that Jack was the person who'd entered her house, but her instincts told her she was right. Mia wasn't sure if Jack knew where Karen lived or not. Fortunately, he had no idea Sasha was staying right in Tarrytown. The thought of him prowling around could send Sasha over the edge. They all needed to be cautious and watch their backs.

Mia asked Aaron to join them for lunch. She'd told Vic about her relationship with Aaron already and it was time for the others to be told, too, especially since Aaron was staying at her house.

They agreed to meet at Amelia's at noon. Mia and Aaron were waiting when everyone showed up. Tina and Karen looked surprised. Vic snickered and grinned.

"What's this about?" Tina asked, laughing. "Can I say it's about damn time, and I love you both?" She air kissed Mia and Aaron as she sat down.

Aaron blushed, stood up, and introduced himself to

Sasha, since she hadn't formally met him yet. Vic hugged him then gave him fair warning. "You mess with my girl, and you'll have me to answer to, mister."

Sasha looked scared. The others broke out laughing and explained that Aaron had been one of them since elementary school.

"We're just goofing around, Sasha. Aaron loves Mia to death and always has."

"Oh good, I wasn't sure what was going on. One freaky guy is enough for me."

"Speaking of freaks," Mia said, "we wanted to talk to all of you about Jack.

"Oh no, now what?" Karen asked.

"There's no proof yet, but I'm pretty sure he's the one with my house key. I'm almost positive he came in Sunday when I was walking Reggie. So, first off, Aaron and I went out that afternoon and bought a spy cam. It's already installed in the bushes right by the front door. We have to catch Jack doing something wrong before we can press charges. Karen, does he know where you live?"

"No, thank God. He probably thinks I live in the city somewhere."

"Good. I doubt if he has any clue you're in Tarrytown, Sasha. Not to sound mean, but Jack would naturally assume this town is beneath you and your standards."

"I guess that's good for me, but I love my new town," she said.

"We know you do, hon. I want all of you to be careful. Luckily, Jack didn't see Vic or Tina that Friday night, so I think you guys are fine. Until this is resolved, Aaron is staying at my house. The app for the camera video feed can go on five different devices. I have one, and Aaron does too. I want Sasha, Karen, and either Tina or Vic to download the app to their phones. Since you guys are at the salon together most of the day, it doesn't matter to me which phone it's on. We can all keep our eyes peeled. As long as Jack doesn't have a job, he can come and go as he pleases. He could be watching me any time, day or night."

"That's so scary," Sasha said. "It gives me chills."

"It will be okay. At the rate he's going, we'll probably catch him this week. Let's order lunch and get on a happier topic like the wedding. I'm sure Vic wants to tell us all about it." Mia winked at her friend.

"That's right, Chica, and do I have a lot to tell." It was apparent by the glow on Vic's face that she was smitten with Max Cole. "He is so hot, and we had such a good time. We stayed until the reception was over. Oh yeah, get this: I caught the bouquet, and Max caught the garter. That has to be a sign, doesn't it? I mean, what are the odds? Next Saturday, we're going on a motorcycle ride to Rhinebeck. Cool huh?"

"That's awesome," Mia said. "Maybe soon you can introduce Max to Aaron. We can all hang out together on weekends and have parties. Good times, right?"

"You bet. Max and Aaron would get along great."

"Well, that sounds good to me. Plus I make killer barbecue chicken on the grill," Aaron said.

Chapter Six

Thursday morning arrived with much-needed rain. Gray skies lingered overhead, and the sound of distant thunder rumbled. Mia and Aaron were burrowed deep beneath the blankets, sound asleep. She jumped from the noise at the foot of the bed.

"Damn it, Reggie—you scared the crap out of me." Reggie whined anxiously. He scratched at the blankets to get Mia up. "Great timing. It's raining like a son of a gun, and you have to go outside? Fine, I'm up."

"Babe, I can walk Reggie—I don't mind. What time is it anyway?"

"It's seven o'clock. You can sleep for another hour." She kissed him and gave his shaft a teasing stroke.

"You're the devil in disguise," he moaned as his erection began to grow.

"No can do, mister," she squealed as Aaron tried to pull her back into bed. "Reggie's going to pee on the floor."

"I'll clean it up—I promise," he pleaded.

"Go back to sleep, you goof. I'll be back in fifteen

minutes."

"Nah… I'm awake now. I'll start the coffee, then you can start me when you get back," he said, giving a dimpled grin.

"What am I going to do with you? Never mind—it's already obvious." Mia slid the rain jacket over her head and grabbed an umbrella. She put the leash on Reggie's collar, and they bolted out into the morning downpour.

Aaron slipped on his sweats and stumbled sleepily into the kitchen to make coffee. He hadn't even poured the water into the coffeemaker yet when he heard the front door open. *Wow, Reggie really had to go.* He reached into the cabinet and pulled out two coffee cups, placing them on the counter. He turned, expecting Mia and Reggie to come around the corner.

His eyes locked onto Jack's, and their bodies froze. Jack turned and ran. Instinct told Aaron to chase him. He caught up with Jack then grabbed him by the arm and wrestled him to the floor in the foyer. They threw wild punches at each other until one of Aaron's connected, tearing into Jack's lip. Jack was cornered against the wall with little opportunity of escape.

***

"C'mon Reggie—hurry up. You're soaked, and I am too. Just go to the bathroom already." Reggie finally did his business, and as Mia rounded the last corner to go home, it sat parked in front of her—Jack's BMW, along the curb a block and a half from her front door. "Oh God, no.

Hurry, Reggie—let's go home." Mia ran as fast as she could with Reggie leading the way. She reached the sidewalk and threw open the front door to find Aaron and Jack in the foyer. Jack sat in the corner against the wall with Aaron hovering above him, blocking the only exit.

"Mia, wait in the kitchen and hang on to Reggie. I've already called the police."

As Mia paced in the kitchen she heard Jack yelling. "You bitch! You ruined my life. My career is gone because of you. You're gonna pay. I swear to God you'll be sorry."

"Shut the hell up, Jack, or I'll shut your mouth myself," Aaron spewed.

"No, Aaron, let me take care of this." Mia furiously stormed toward Jack. "You've been a piece of shit and wasted three years of my life. You treated me like dirt and cheated on me the entire time. All I ever wanted was to be happily married and have a family. You made sure that would never happen. You're cruel and arrogant. You're nothing but a loser—always have been and always will be. The only thing you deserve is this." Mia wound up and slapped Jack across the face as hard as she could. His cheek welted red immediately.

"Don't even try it," Aaron said as Jack started to get up.

The blaring sound of sirens got closer. Two squad cars pulled up in front of Mia's house. Two officers of the Tarrytown police department came inside. "Mia, Jack, Aaron, what's going on here?" Officer Owens asked.

Mia explained that she and Jack were divorcing, how

she'd changed all the locks, and how Jack had sneaked in and stolen her spare house key. In addition to trespassing, he'd threatened her. She wanted to press charges against him, and she also wanted an order of protection filed.

"Jack, empty your pockets," Officer Lenard said. Jack did, and on his own key ring was Mia's spare house key. "Okay, let's go. We're taking you downtown for booking. Mia and Aaron, you need to come along and give your statements. Mia, you'll have to sign some paperwork." The officer handcuffed Jack's hands behind his back, read him his rights, and took him away.

"Oh my God, Aaron—I'm so relieved you're okay," Mia said, her voice trembling. "I saw Jack's car parked a few blocks away and could only imagine the worst."

"It's okay now, honey." Aaron held her and stroked her hair. "Where did you get such a good arm? Holy cow, woman—you really wound up on that one." He shook his head in amazement.

"You don't remember high school? The girls' softball team went to the state finals. I was the pitcher."

"What am I going to do with you?"

"I'll show you tonight," she said teasingly. "Right now, it looks like we have to make a statement. What are you going to do about the shop?"

"I'll call my dad. He can open this morning and take care of things for a few hours. Let's go and get this over with."

***

The process downtown took several hours. Red tape seemed to drag things out. Jack was finally booked and had to stay in jail, awaiting his hearing. Mia was relieved. If Jack violated the restraining order, he'd be back in jail. She hoped it would all end soon, and Jack would get on with his life somewhere else.

Aaron was finally allowed to leave the police station and go to work at ten thirty. "I guess they're done with me. Stop by the shop later if you aren't busy, okay?"

"Sure. I'm going to call Karen and see if she and Sasha want to have lunch. I'll stop by after that. I love you, and thanks for protecting me. I don't know if Jack would have done anything or not, but I'm glad you were there. You're my hero."

"I like the sound of that. Can you drop me off, or do I have to walk in this downpour?"

When Mia dropped Aaron off at the front door of his shop, the senior Mr. Daniels was standing behind the counter, helping a customer.

"I guess we'll have to tell your dad what's going on pretty soon," Mia said as Aaron exited the car. She gave him a kiss and drove back home.

She entered the kitchen and stared. The coffee carafe, filled with water, sat on the counter. Two mugs waited for the hot brew that never happened. It was as if time had stopped. Mia exhaled with a sigh. *What a crazy morning. I need some decent coffee instead the garbage at the police station.* She poured four cups of water into the reservoir and two heaping scoops of Starbucks Columbian Roast into the filter, then toasted two slices of raisin bread. She sat at the table and nibbled while she called Karen.

"Hey, Mia, what's up?"

"You wouldn't even believe it. Are you busy today? I was thinking about lunch. I want to invite Sasha, too."

"That's a nice gesture. I think she would enjoy getting to know you and me better. It doesn't always have to include Tina and Vic."

"That's what I think, too. Do you want to come here, or should we come to Greenwich?"

"Sasha has never been to my house. There's some great restaurants downtown. Come here, okay? How about twelve thirty?"

"That sounds great. Is it raining there?"

"This morning it was, but it looks like it's breaking up. I see blue sky now."

"Good. That should make for a nicer day. I'll pick up Sasha, and we'll see you in a few hours."

Mia called Sasha as she washed down the last bite of cinnamon raisin toast with coffee. "Hey, Sasha, do you want to have lunch with Karen and me today?"

"But it's Thursday. I thought we only got together on Tuesdays when the salon was closed, and usually we all have lunch together."

"Honey, I don't want you to be embarrassed around Karen and me. We can have lunch whenever we want even when Vic and Tina aren't with us. We're all friends, remember?"

"I know, but my guilty conscience takes over

sometimes."

"That will go away," Mia said. "It's just been a few weeks. We're good… really. All of us are better off without Jack in our lives. We did each other a favor."

"If I look at it that way, I do feel better. Okay, let's do lunch."

"That's my girl. I'll pick you up at noon. We're going to Greenwich. Cool, huh? You can see where Karen lives."

"That sounds exciting. I'll see you at noon," Sasha said. "Mia?"

"Yes?"

"Thank you for forgiving me and being my friend."

"Stop it before I start crying. I'll honk when I'm outside. See you soon."

Mia noticed a group of newspaper stands along the front of the grocery store a few minutes from Tina's house. She pulled in and parked her car. She grabbed three *Realtor* magazines to give Sasha. Sasha had accepted the offer on her apartment, and it was time to go house hunting. They would all pitch in and help her find a place in Tarrytown. It would be fun looking for the perfect house in a great neighborhood. Sasha would need to tell them what she liked. Would she prefer modern or vintage? Did she want a house or a condo? *We can talk about it while we drive to Karen's house. I wonder if Karen has thought about moving to Tarrytown now that we're all friends. Greenwich is so expensive.*

Mia pulled into the driveway and beeped the horn twice and Sasha came out, looking amazing. *She would be beautiful wearing a burlap bag. How does she do it? Must be good genes.* Sasha jumped into the passenger seat, a pleased expression on her face.

"What?" Mia asked as she drove.

"What do you mean *what*?"

"Okay, I should have said, why?"

"Why what?" Sasha asked, completely perplexed.

Mia burst out laughing. "You're completely clueless, aren't you?"

"About what?"

"I don't know. You have a childlike innocence about you, yet you're a successful model with everything going for you. Then you hook up with Jack? Who is the real Sasha anyway? Are you the Sasha we know or the Sasha Jack knew?"

"Are you mad at me?"

"No, honey, I just want to know the real you. Remember how you acted the day we met you at the salon? You were a spoiled brat. But then there was the Sasha I ran into at the train station. She was a caring, sweet woman even though I was a basket case that day. You seem so happy and carefree now. I just want to know if it's real or if you're doing it for our benefit?"

"It's real, Mia. Remember when I wrote that note on the dollar bill?"

"Yes, I do."

"Well, somehow, even though I didn't know you guys more than a few hours, I knew my life was about to change, like something good was going to happen, and it did. Look at the four of you. I have real friends now, not the superficial model crowd that gossips when someone has a zit or gains five pounds. You guys are real. You're my true friends even after what I did with Jack. I'm so sorry about that. I didn't know about you—I really didn't."

"It's okay. Jack used all of us. Anyway, I'll tell you the news about him at lunch. Karen has to hear it, too. Reach over the backseat. I grabbed some real estate magazines for you to browse through. We need to go house hunting, girl." Mia smiled and squeezed Sasha's hand. "We're good. Don't worry about it anymore."

Chapter Seven

The Camaro roared into the driveway of the Cape Cod. "Here we are. Cute place isn't it?" Mia said.

"I love it. This is kind of what I'm looking for."

"So, you like the traditional style? You're more into the old than the new?"

"Of course. Tarrytown is a quaint village with beautiful older homes. If I wanted something modern, I'd stay in the city. I like the settled-in look, something comfortable, a place with a story all its own."

Mia smiled. "I get what you mean. We'll find you a beautiful older home. Remind me to show you Aaron's house. You'll fall in love with it. C'mon—let's go in."

Karen welcomed Sasha and Mia inside. A large pitcher of iced tea and three glasses sat on the rattan table on the patio. "Let me show you the house, Sasha, then we'll have some tea before we leave for lunch. I decided on Katzen Kafe. It's a cute place downtown."

"Your home is so beautiful," Sasha said. "Will you help pick out a house for me? You have great taste."

"Sure, that sounds like fun." Karen introduced her to

Claire and briefly told Sasha the story Jack had concocted about the cat. Sasha shook her head in disbelief. "I can't understand that man. He's quite the liar isn't he?"

"Um… yeah," Mia said. "Let's go outside and enjoy that iced tea. I have something to tell you both about Jack that will definitely floor you."

They made themselves comfortable on the floral cushions covering the chairs. As Karen poured iced tea, Mia began. "You guys remember me telling you how someone stole my spare house key, right?"

"Yep," Karen said as she stirred a teaspoon of sugar into her tea.

"Then we thought it was Jack, so we got the spy cam."

"Right."

"It was Jack," Mia said.

"What?" Karen and Sasha yelled simultaneously.

Mia told them the story of taking Reggie for a walk in the rain and coming home to find Jack. "Aaron called the police just before I got back to the house. The cops took Jack away. I filed charges against him for trespassing, plus I filed for an order of protection."

"Oh my God—you're both okay, right?" Karen said.

"Yeah, we're fine. I'm really relieved this is over though. You two shouldn't worry about Jack since he has no idea where you guys live. Plus he might finally have learned that he has to move on and leave all of us alone."

"Amen to that," Karen said. "I wonder if Jack had a plan, sneaking in like that."

"Who knows? I can't picture him being physically

violent, but his job meant everything to him, so I couldn't say for sure. Anyway, it's over and done with. I just wanted to tell you guys. I'll keep you posted on everything that goes on with this. I mean, even though we're still married, the house has always been in my name only. I gave him fair warning that we were over, not to come back, and that I was changing the locks. So, I'm pretty sure the trespassing charges will stick."

"Thanks, Mia. I'm so happy Jack is out of our lives. Do you think there are some nice guys in Tarrytown I might meet someday?" Sasha asked.

"Of course, hon. Aaron has nice friends, plus some of the business owners' downtown are single. Tarrytown is a great place to live and raise a family if that's your plan."

"Oh, it is… eventually. Should we go have lunch?"

"Yeah, let's go," Karen said.

***

Mia stopped at the camera shop on her way home. The police had returned the spare key to her, so she wanted to make sure it was in Aaron's reliable hands.

"How was lunch with the girls?"

"Pretty good. I told them about Jack. I could see by the look on their faces they were relieved he was caught. I hope this situation will make him think twice about doing something so stupid again. Anyway, here's the spare key. It's the only one, and you should keep it."

"Thanks, honey. Does that mean I'm welcome anytime?"

"Of course it does, as long as you don't sneak up on

me."

"I promise I won't. I'll be over after work. I can pick something up at the grocery store if you want me to."

Mia laughed. "Listen to us. We sound like a real couple already. I like it. No… I love it, and I love you."

"I love you, too. Call if you want me to grab a few things later."

**

The bell above the door jingled as Mia walked out. She looked back through the window, smiling, and blew Aaron a kiss before she disappeared around the corner.

My God, how did I get so lucky? I finally have the woman I've loved for almost twenty years. Aaron grinned and went back to work.

The chimes on Mia's grandfather's clock rang out six times when Aaron opened the front door with his own key. It felt right. His mind drifted back to earlier that morning. So much had happened, and yet it was still the same day. *Unbelievable.* He set the groceries on the kitchen counter. Aaron didn't want to startle Mia, so he called out to her. He heard the sound of the shower running in the master bathroom.

"I'm taking a shower," she said. "I'll be out in a few minutes."

"Would you like some company? I'm suddenly feeling very dirty."

"You're crazy. Of course I would love some company. Get in here and wash my back."

"Gladly." Aaron stripped and entered the large, steaming shower. He took the washcloth from her hand and lathered it up with soap. Mia's knotted shoulders and back relaxed as Aaron kneaded them with the soapy cloth. She turned to face him. He looked her over longingly and smiled as he continued. He cupped her breasts in his hands as he gently caressed each one. Their kisses were long and passionate. Aaron continued downward with the lathered washcloth. Mia's body stiffened when he reached that perfect spot. Aaron licked and flicked her nipples with his tongue as he pressed his growing shaft against her belly. Mia moaned in ecstasy.

"Aaron, I want you."

"I'm here for you, babe." Aaron lowered himself on the tiled shower seat while Mia straddled his legs. She slowly inched herself down onto his hard, throbbing shaft while she kissed his neck and nuzzled his earlobes.

"You drive me crazy." Aaron whispered his desire for his blond beauty. He thrust his shaft into her as she bore down on it.

Mia rode him until they both exploded in an orgasmic frenzy.

***

Vic paced the floor with nervous energy. Tomorrow, she would be spending the entire day with Max. She'd never thought much about having a serious boyfriend. It had never mattered to her one way or another. She already had the best friends in the world and a huge extended family.

She was fine with that and completely content in her singleness. Now, Max Cole was in the picture, and she liked him a lot. Vic had dated occasionally, but she'd never before had the perfect man handed to her on a silver platter. She had no idea what to do with him. She felt insecure with such a gorgeous guy.

I've got to talk to Mia. I'll see if she wants to do lunch. It was still early, only eight o'clock, but Vic couldn't wait any longer to call Mia. "Hey, Chica, do you want to do lunch today, just the two of us?"

"Sure. I have a family portrait at ten, but noon is fine. It's a local family anyway, so I'll be in town. What's up? Why not invite Tina?"

"We need to talk about Max. I told you we're taking his Harley to Rhinebeck tomorrow, right?"

"Yep, I remember you saying that. It should be a lot of fun," Mia said. Vic could hear her sipping her coffee.

"I know, but… well, we just have to talk first."

"Okay, no problem. When and where?"

At noon, Vic waited anxiously at the long, dark, bar just inside the door at Morey's, where they had agreed to meet. Vic made the usual small talk with Morey while she stared absentmindedly at the menu. She knew it by heart, as well as Friday's fish-fry special, but food didn't matter right at the moment. With her nerves out of control, she had to talk to Mia. Vic gulped down a glass of ice water and asked Morey for another. Her foot bounced up and down against the bar rail. She breathed a sigh of relief when she saw Mia park outside and come through the door.

"Let's get a table, okay?" Vic said.

"Sure. Hey, Morey, we're grabbing a table over here."

"Yeah, Mia—no problem, I'll be there in a minute," he yelled back from the kitchen.

"What's got you all twisted up?" Mia asked.

"I don't know. Something must be wrong with me. The hottest guy on the planet wants to hang out with me for the entire day tomorrow, and I'm freaking out."

"What the hell for?" Mia took off her sunglasses and set the menu down.

"Because *he* asked me out. He went to my cousin's wedding with me because I kind of insisted. He agreed out of pity."

"Are you out of your friggin' mind? Why would you even say that?"

"Mia, look at yourself. You were with him first. I'm the runner-up, the consolation prize... if that. He is way too hot to honestly be interested in me." Vic looked around for Morey to take their order. "Should we get a bottle of wine?"

"Sure, hon." Mia yelled, "Morey, get out here and take our order. Bring me a pan to whack Vic over the head with, too."

"Mia, jeez!"

"Max likes you a lot. Why are you being so insecure right now? Haven't you looked in the mirror lately? You're hotter than shit. I can see that, and he can, too. Every available guy in Westchester County can see that, for crap's sake. Come on—what's really going on? You're the most full-of-yourself babe I know. If it's about Max and me, I'm going to slap you right now, I swear."

"But…"

"But nothing. How many times in our lives have we gone out with the same guy at one time or another? Shit like that happens, especially when you live in a small town. Honey, I'm in love with Aaron. He's going to be the man I marry. Max and I had thirty-six hours of horny hormones going nuts between us. We both get that, and I want to remain friends with him, but only if we're all in agreement. It would be awesome if you guys became more, and Max knows I love Aaron. He asked you to spend the day with him tomorrow because he likes you. Since when have you ever been insecure?"

"I don't know. Maybe I don't even want a boyfriend. I'd have to watch Max every second, as hot as he is. Every girl in a fifty-mile radius would be trying to get in his pants."

"He is a diamond in the rough and has no idea how hot he is. That is, except from us. We tell him all the time. Max is a few years older than we are. He doesn't have a girlfriend, he's never been married, and he does field trips with the Boy Scouts. He might be ready to get involved with somebody. Timing is everything, and maybe it's time. *What will be, will be. See where it goes,* and all those stupid clichés. Really, Vic, go out and enjoy the day tomorrow. If there's another date planned, see what happens. Wouldn't it be great if all of us ended up coupled with someone? We could live in Tarrytown forever and raise our kids together. We'd have barbecues every weekend and pool parties."

"Who has a pool?" Vic asked with a pout.

"Nobody yet, you dummy, but in a few years, somebody might. C'mon, let's order. I'm hungry."

Chapter Eight

She couldn't sleep. The reassurance Mia had given her at lunch still didn't settle Vic's nerves. *What is it about Max that has me so insecure? We had a great time at the wedding, flirting and all. But now? Does he like me, or does he only want to date me to be close to Mia?* She glanced at the clock on the nightstand—2:14 a.m. She stumbled to the kitchen, overtired and irritated. A cup of Sleepytime tea might calm her nerves. She plopped down on the recliner and clicked the remote, flipping through the channels in search of something boring enough to help her fall asleep. She stopped at PBS, which was broadcasting a segment about shutting down fisheries to protect the tuna population. *This should do it for me.* She sipped her tea. Within thirty minutes, she was back in bed.

The annoying alarm set for eight o'clock blasted in Vic's ears. She reached up to ride the snooze button, peeking through her slits of barely-open eyes, and saw it was nine o'clock. "Son of a bitch," she shrieked as she jumped out of bed. "I should have been up an hour ago. Max is going to be here at ten."

Vic tossed a cup of water into the microwave and grabbed the instant coffee from the pantry. *Shit. When was the last time I used this?* She looked at the expiration date on the jar. It read "Expires 6-14-09." *Damn it! What the hell? Stale coffee isn't going to kill me. Reminder to self— clean out the pantry sometime soon.* She didn't have much time, so she had to improvise with her looks. *We'll be on his motorcycle anyway. No reason to worry about my hair. I'll have helmet head all day the way it is.* She showered and spritzed on Chanel. Glossing her unruly, long, dark hair into a sleek braid would be her only option. *Thank God it's a motorcycle date. There's no time to fart around with my hair anyway.* Vic applied a small amount of makeup then slipped on a pair of tight jeans, a tank top, and her moto boots. She checked herself in the mirror as she guzzled down the lukewarm coffee and ate two Double Stuff Oreo cookies.

The deep throttling sound of the Harley was unmistakable as it pulled into her driveway. Her heart pounded, and her palms were sweaty. *Oh my God—knock it off, and take a deep breath. If Max reaches for my hand and feels how sweaty it is, he's going to be so grossed out.* He knocked on the door. Vic did another quick look in the mirror. *Okay… I'm cool, and I look awesome.* She took a deep breath, pulled the confident persona out of the closet, and opened the front door.

"Hey, hot stuff," Max said with a smile spreading across his entire face. "Are you ready to make my day?"

"Max, you're crazy." *He actually looks happy to see me.*

"Today is going to be a blast."

"You seem different."

"Oh shit… I'm sorry. I woke up late and didn't have a lot of time to get dolled up."

"No, I didn't mean it in a bad way. It's a compliment. I really like that subtle style. I'm a small-town guy. You were drop-dead gorgeous at the wedding, don't get me wrong, but today, you're even more beautiful."

Vic felt her face heat up. The blush had to be evident to Max.

"I didn't mean to embarrass you. I only wanted to say you look really nice."

"Thanks. You're not too bad yourself," she responded, back to true form—her usual fun-loving cockiness.

"That's my girl. Let's go have a great motorcycle ride."

Vic finally let her guard down and smiled. *Max just might be the real deal after all.* "Hell yeah, I'm not wearing these boots for nothing when it's eighty degrees outside. I even borrowed a leather biker jacket, too." She laughed.

"All right, gorgeous, let's go. Here, put on this helmet. We don't want anything happening to that beautiful head of yours." Max caught her off guard when he leaned in and kissed her fully on the lips. It was the last thing she expected, but she wrapped her arms around his neck and responded eagerly.

"Let's go before we change our minds and stay here," she said, taken aback—but very turned on.

"You got it. Rhinebeck, here we come."

The ride to Rhinebeck took an hour and a half. Max

drove his Harley through small towns and winding roads along the Hudson River on Route 9. The weather was perfect with a cloudless blue sky and a light breeze. They weaved in and out of the shadows of large trees along the route.

Vic wrapped her arms tightly around Max's strong, muscular torso. She inhaled the woodsy, spicy scent of Gucci Pour Homme on his shirt as she snuggled in close. *Oh my God, I've died and gone to heaven. This man is going to drive me insane, I swear.*

They parked near the Beekman Arms and walked through the shopping districts along East Market Street and Montgomery. Each gallery and antique store was more interesting than the one before.

Lunch at the Public House was a fun experience all its own. Max started the conversation as they waited for their salmon burger and catfish tacos to be served. "So, other than owning Hair Brained with Tina, what's your story? I want to know everything about you. You piqued my interest from the minute you came rushing out of Mia's house yelling at us." Max let out a full-blown laugh.

"I'm sorry your first impression of me was of some whack job ready to attack you both. In hindsight, it's kind of funny, but then, I was really worried about Mia."

"There's something special about you girls. You love each other and have a bond nobody will ever come between. I like that about all of you... you're loyal. That says quite a bit about your personalities. It's an admirable quality."

"Do you have a group of close friends?" she asked.

"Nah… not anymore. I used to, back in the day. I don't ride with those types any longer. I'd much rather ride with a beautiful woman like you."

"Thanks. That's a nice thing to say. As far as myself, I never really found someone that took my breath away. I've been perfectly content living my life as it's been for years. I have a great group of friends, and you saw how huge my family is." Vic chuckled. "But I'm thirty-three years old. If I am going to do anything different with my life, I guess I should start giving it some thought."

"I get what you're saying. I'm kind of in the same boat. I love kids but never had any of my own. Haven't met the right gal. It's not good to stop looking though. Life can pass you by, and before you know it, you've lost the opportunity to get married and have a family."

"Do you want that for yourself?"

"Sure I do. I think I need to start spending more time around adults—of the female gender I mean. I love the Boy Scouts and camping—it's a great life being a wilderness guide—but not if I ever plan to have a family of my own."

"What would you do for a living if you weren't a guide?"

"I've always thought of opening my own hiking and camping supply store. I think it would go over well in this neck of the woods."

"Wow, that's ambitious. I think it could be a great success. There's nothing like that around us—in

Tarrytown, I mean." She looked at Max, sure that he could read her thoughts.

"I don't live in Tarrytown, Vic."

"But you could."

Vic and Max were connecting with no expectations other than having a wonderful day together. They talked a lot, browsed the shops, and walked hand in hand. They learned a lot about each other at lunch. The day held magical possibilities. Riding back to Tarrytown was relaxing yet playful. Along the Hudson River, they stopped and took in some of the sights. They walked through the Sleepy Hollow Cemetery just because Max had never seen the burial site of Washington Irving.

They arrived back in Tarrytown at six thirty, just in time for dinner. Eating at Bottoms Up was a great way to end their perfect day. They sat outside on the patio after dinner, Max with a mug of beer and Vic with a glass of wine.

"I want you to know how much I enjoyed today." Vic sipped Merlot as she studied Max and took in his features. He was gorgeous. She couldn't find anything remotely wrong with him. "So, what's with all the tattoos? I really like tats and even have a few myself, but yours don't seem to fit your personality. I picture them on someone with a rougher edge. You're thoughtful and such a gentleman."

Max laughed. "What? The grim reaper and skull and crossbones don't fit my personality? That image used to be me a long time ago. But that's a story for another time. Should we head out?"

"Sure, let's go."

Vic had enjoyed Max's company so much that she hated to end the day. As she got off the bike in front of her house, she asked, "Do you want to come in for a bit before you go home? I can whip together a few cups of coffee." She was hoping he would say yes.

"Aren't you sick of me yet?"

"Not even close. C'mon in. At least have some coffee for the road."

"Okay. You're the boss."

Vic poured two large mugs of Columbian roast. "Do you take cream or sugar?" She reached into the refrigerator for the cream.

"Just cream, thanks."

She flashed Max a smile as she closed the refrigerator door. "Same way I take it. No wonder I like you—we have a lot in common." Vic set the cups on saucers with stirring spoons and brought them to the table where Max sat.

"So, I did good today?" he asked, giving her a wink. "I want to make sure there's a chance for another date with you, Vic. I don't want to screw it up."

"Are you ready for this—dating, I mean?"

"Yeah… I think I am. It feels good. I like spending time with you. I hope you feel the same."

Vic leaned in and kissed him. "I'd love to go out with you again. Maybe we're both seeing there's more to life than just our jobs and closest friends. To be honest, this is the first actual date I've gone on in three years."

"So, the wedding didn't count?"

"Sure, if you consider you, me, and two hundred of my friends and family a date," she said, laughing. "No, I mean just two people, alone together for the entire day. That's a date, and today was a real date."

She walked Max out to his Harley. It was already nine o'clock, and he still had a half hour drive home. "Thanks, again."

Max stood next to his bike, fidgeting with the keys. "Vic, can I call you this week?"

"Of course, you can. I'd love to talk to you, or see you, anytime."

"Good. That's exactly what I wanted to hear. Good night." Max took her face in his hands and kissed her softly at first, then more deeply. They both wanted more, but there would be time for that later. This was a special moment to enjoy just the way it was.

Chapter Nine

Mia was taking a bite of the grilled ham-and-cheese sandwich when her cell phone rang. "Damn it," she muttered with a full mouth, trying to swallow quickly and clear her throat to speak. "Hello?"

"Ms. James, this is the county clerk calling from the courthouse in White Plains. Your husband, Jack Barnes, is due in court on Wednesday. We're calling to say that you and anyone else involved have the right to appear and make a victim's statement. His arraignment is at one o'clock in courtroom 7B."

"Oh… okay. Thank you. I'll give that some consideration." Mia hung up and immediately called Aaron. "What should we do?"

"Go ahead and make a statement. Jack has to realize that you're a strong woman and won't play his game anymore. You need to say your piece, and I do too, for that matter. He has to see we won't tolerate his bullying and scare tactics. What's your opinion?"

"I agree—we should do it. I want to show the judge we're taking this seriously. I don't want Jack in my life, or around my house, ever again."

"Good answer. I'm proud of you, honey. Why don't you and Reggie spend the night tonight? I'll whip up a nice dinner for us, then we can go for a leisurely walk around the neighborhood."

"That sounds great. One of these days, we're going to have to talk about putting my house up for sale," Mia said.

"Wow... that's a committed statement. I like where this is going. Let's discuss it later over dinner and wine."

"That sounds nice. Bye, Aaron."

"Bye, sweetheart."

***

Vic talked a mile a minute as she trimmed and highlighted Mrs. Johnson's hair. She wanted everyone to hear about her date with Max. The ladies in the salon listened with their ears perked up, ready to offer their two cents. Stacy Hill said Vic should have let Max spend the night. Mrs. Johnson thought they should have set up the next date before he left. Vic enjoyed the banter, especially since she was the center of attention.

Tina was quick to describe Max to all the gray-haired ladies and hipsters in the salon, just to get them going. "If you ladies had any idea how hot this guy of Vic's is, you'd be blown away. I mean, I've never seen a man as sexy as him in my life. He has muscles pouring out of every limb—and I do mean *every!*" Tina laughed when Vic gave her a look of utter shock. The old ladies gasped at the comment, and the hipsters salivated.

"Well… all I can say is I'm anxious to go out with him again. He just might stay overnight, Stacy. Who knows what a little wine will do?" Vic smirked as she looked over at Tina. They both enjoyed giving the customers something to chatter about. The salon was known as the hot gossip spot of Tarrytown.

Hair Brained closed at five o'clock. Vic and Tina stopped at Bottoms Up to have a glass of wine together and talk privately.

"I've never seen you this giddy. You act like a different person. I mean, you're Vic, always cutting up and goofy, but now you're super happy."

"I'm usually happy, but this is a different kind of happy. It's like I have something to look forward to."

"That's great. And Max—how does he seem?"

"He was behaving the same way. We kissed, and he complimented me, like, a million times. He said he's looking forward to our next date and asked if he could call me during the week. I've never been around a guy as polite as him. What's *that* about? I've never even met girls that nice."

"Who knows? Just enjoy it, sister."

Vic went home alone with a lot on her mind. She needed to test Max to find out if he was sincere about his feelings for her. *Is it really about me, or is it just a way to stay close to Mia? Damn it—why did he and Mia ever meet at all?* Vic didn't like feeling insecure, and it wasn't her norm. But the woman in question was Mia, the blond beauty everyone adored, and not some fleabag gutter skank. And Max? He was the true Adonis of the northeast.

Vic decided to plan a party. She'd say it was in honor of Mia and Aaron becoming a couple. Everyone would be invited, including Max. She had to see if Max was truly into her or Mia, even though it seemed like a sneaky, underhanded way to find out. No matter what, Mia was Vic's best friend for life. *Relationships come and go, but Mia and I are like sisters. Nobody will ever come between us, not even the hottest guy on earth.*

Vic entered her bedroom and opened the closet door. The back side held a full-length mirror. She stripped off her clothes and stared at herself the way a man would look at a naked woman. She studied her body closely. *My figure is okay—curvy, but not too curvy. My ass is big, but I am Puerto Rican, for God's sake. Anyone would understand that. My boobs are nice—no kids, so they don't droop yet. I have a tiny waist, and that's a plus.* She studied her face and teeth in the mirror, up close and critical. She smiled, mouth open and mouth closed, to see which way looked better. *I have great teeth, so I should show them when I smile. Shit! When I smile with my mouth closed, my eyes squint. I wonder how long I've been doing that! My eyes are gorgeous, I must admit.* She opened her eyes wide and studied the gold-colored flecks sprinkled throughout her stunning green irises. Her eyelashes were thick and long. *I should practice batting my eyes.* She moved on to her hair. *Well… there isn't much I can do with these kinky curls. I guess I need to accept them. On a positive note, my hair is long and full. No split ends. The curls are healthy and shiny. Okay, my hair gets an A plus, at least when the humidity doesn't turn the entire mop to frizz. Would I think I was hot if I were a guy?* An idea popped into her head as she put her clothes back on, and she called Mia.

"Chica, I gotta talk to you about a few things. Is Aaron with you?"

"Yeah, I'm at his place. We're making dinner. Why?"

"Ask him if he thinks I'm hot." Vic put Mia on speakerphone and began plucking her eyebrows in the bathroom mirror.

"What?"

"No, seriously—please ask him." Vic plucked while she waited.

"Just a minute. By the way, Vic, you're a total head case. Aaron?"

"Yes, what is it babe?"

"Vic wants to know if you think she's hot." Mia began giggling.

Vic could only imagine the expression on Aaron's face.

His voice in the background said, "Um… what am I supposed to say? Is this a trick question with a right and wrong answer? I'm sure this is against the man code."

"Oh for God's sake, Mia, just tell him to answer you honestly. Nobody is going to give a shit, and you aren't going to get mad at his answer anyway."

"So, you're assuming he's going to say yes?" Mia teased.

"Damn it already—put his ass on the phone."

"Aaron, Vic wants to talk to you." Mia was laughing so

hard her words came out in giggles.

"Hello, Vic," he said apprehensively.

"Aaron, grow a set already. I've known you since we were in grade school for crap's sake. Am I hot or not? I want a guy's opinion, and I think you're a guy, aren't you?"

"Yeah… I mean, of course I am. Jeez, Vic, nothing like putting me on the spot—thanks. So, you want me to answer right in front of Mia?"

"Duh! Just answer my friggin' question already."

"Okay. Yes, you're hot. Are you happy now?"

"Yep. Thanks. Put Mia back on the phone."

Mia was still laughing when she came back on the line. "Hey, thanks for freaking him out."

"Well, what the hell… seriously? Anyway, I want to plan a coming-out party."

"Is there something more you're trying to tell me?" Mia squealed with laughter.

"I mean for you guys, as a couple, you dork. That kind of coming-out party. So, I have to start planning it. How about Saturday, August 23? I mean, by now people have seen you around town together, and our friends know you're a couple. What do you say? We'll have the party at my house. I haven't thrown a party in years. Ask Aaron if his dad can cover the shop that day and get back to me. I don't have much time to put this together. Call me tomorrow and let me know. Out."

***

"You know she's certifiable, right?" Aaron said as he set the table.

Mia went back to tossing the salad. She wiped her eyes with her sleeve. "Oh, she definitely is, but I love her anyway."

Chapter Ten

Mia stared out the car window Wednesday as Aaron drove I-278 east to White Plains. The courthouse wasn't far enough for her to sink deep in thought, being only a fifteen-minute ride door to door. But she wasn't the chipper Mia he was accustomed to.

"Are you nervous, honey?" He reached for her hand.

"I guess I am. Aren't you?"

He glanced at Mia, trying to read her thoughts. "It's uncomfortable, but it's something we need to do. Jack has to be held accountable. He wanted to terrorize you, and he succeeded. I'm just glad it was cut short before anything dangerous happened."

"Do you think Jack is dangerous?" Mia shuddered, giving the idea too much thought.

"I don't know, honey, but he certainly didn't have the right to do what he did. All we need to say is that he violated your rights as a home owner and trespassed on your private property. His offense is like breaking and entering except he stole the key, so he didn't actually have to break in. If you're afraid to talk, I can say everything that needs to be said. It's all right—I can take care of it."

"I've got to say something. If I don't, Jack wins. He'll know he scared me off. I can't let him victimize me like that."

"I'm proud of you, Mia. Put on a brave face, and he'll never know you're nervous."

They reached the courthouse at twelve forty-five. The beautiful brass retro-style elevator took them to the seventh floor. They found courtroom 7B and peeked in through the heavy oak double doors. The previous case was just finishing up. They quietly slipped in and sat on the last bench by the door. For a few minutes, Mia's mind wandered away from the task ahead of her. She had never been to the courthouse before and was surprised at how beautiful the room was. Carved golden oak adorned every bench. The ornate hanging lamps looked like late-nineteenth-century converted gaslights. An enormous oil-painted mural on the wall behind the judge's bench appeared to be White Plains, probably in the late 1800s. Mia took it all in, being one to spot beauty wherever she was, and relaxed for a few minutes. Aaron nudged her when Jack was led into the room. The anxiety returned.

"Take a deep breath," he said quietly. "I'll go first if that helps."

"Thanks, but I can do this."

The judge read the charges against Jack and asked for his plea. His attorney cupped his hand and whispered in Jack's ear.

Jack reluctantly rose and responded, "No contest." He

sat again.

The judge pushed the bridge of his glasses up higher on his nose and looked over the paperwork. "Is there anyone here who would like to make a victim's statement?" he asked, looking at the people seated in the gallery.

"Yes, your honor." Mia stood. She trembled at the thought of walking to the podium—which in this moment seemed to be miles away—with Jack's eyes laser beamed on her. Yet she did, projecting as much confidence as possible. She knew her appearance was well polished and professional, having dressed carefully that day. Her hair was pulled back in a chignon, and she wore a navy pencil skirt, white blouse, and low navy pumps. She stood at the podium and gave her statement without wavering or looking at Jack. She wouldn't give him the time of day or the satisfaction of seeing fear in her eyes. Aaron rose next and described how Jack had watched the house like a stalker then came in when Mia left.

With a crack of the gavel, the ruling was over, and Jack received six months of probation and two hundred hours of community service. He was also fined, and the order of protection was put into place. He had to stay away from the house and Mia for a year. There could be no emails, phone calls, texts, stalking, or any means of contact. Jack would be back in court with serious charges filed against him if he violated the order. Their divorce would proceed, but any correspondence from Jack would have to go through Mia's divorce attorney.

"Are you happy with the outcome, honey?" Aaron

asked as they drove back to Tarrytown.

"Yes, I am, and I'm glad it's over. We can go on with our life now, hopefully, stress free."

"I like that idea. How about a late lunch? We can go anywhere you want."

"That sounds good. My stomach isn't in knots anymore, and I'm actually hungry. Let's go to Amelia's."

"You got it, babe."

***

The loud Mexican music coming from Vic's purse irritated her to no end. Once again, she'd forgotten to remove the phone before throwing her purse on the floor behind her seat. She swatted at the floor but couldn't reach the purse. She pulled over to avoid swerving into the wrong lane as she twisted her body around the driver's seat, feeling for her purse on the floor. "Hello—Vic speaking," she said, grabbing her phone in the nick of time.

"Vic? Glad I caught you. It's Max. What's up?"

"Max—hi!" *Damn it, Vic. Take it down a few octaves so you don't sound desperate.* "I'm good. How are you?"

"I'm good, too. Hey, I realize it's last minute, but it's such a warm evening. I'd love to pick you up on the bike and take you out to dinner. You haven't eaten yet, have you?"

"No, I'm on my way home from work right now."

"So, how about it? I can be at your place in forty-five minutes. It's the perfect night for a motorcycle ride. We can buzz around town then find a nice spot for dinner."

"That sounds like fun. Okay, you have a deal, but I get to pick the restaurant."

"I wouldn't have it any other way. See you in a few."

I'm really beginning to enjoy this dating thing, Vic thought, as she tried to hit every green light on Main Street. She got home, switched into something sexy—but not too obvious—and freshened up her hair and makeup. *Keep it low-key.* She pulled her hair back into a ponytail and swapped out her pendant earrings for some simple gold studs. She checked herself in the bedroom mirror, making sure she looked wholesome, but a little sexy, in her denim shorts and hot-pink tank top. "Okay, this is perfect. He'll like this look." She brushed her teeth, gargled with mouthwash, and applied lip gloss as she heard the Harley pulling into her driveway.

"Yay—he's here." Staying cool and collected was difficult when just seeing Max increased her heartbeat to an alarming rate. *It's gotta be those damn hormones.* She took her time getting to the front door when he knocked. *I can't appear overly anxious.* She casually opened the door and smiled at the delectable piece of eye candy standing on her porch. *Oh my God, you are the sexiest hunk of manflesh I have ever seen.*

He stood there, smiling. He wore nothing more than a thin white V-neck tee and faded jeans that were extra tight in all the right spots. His deep-brown, wavy hair was wind whipped, making him look deliciously rebellious.

"C'mon in. What a fun surprise—a midweek visit from

you."

"Wow, you're beautiful, Vic. I've thought about you a lot since Saturday. That was a great day. I hope we can have more like that."

"Really?" She threw her purse over her shoulder and jammed the house keys into her pocket.

"Of course, really. Are you having doubts?"

"No, not at all."

"Then come here." Max gave her that gorgeous come-hither dimpled smile that made her knees weak.

Holy shit, he makes my whole body shake. Oh yeah, smile back with my teeth showing. No squinty-eyed smiles. "Is there something I can do for you, Max?" she asked, trying to be coy.

"Sure. You can give me a hello kiss."

Vic kissed Max softly then pulled back teasingly. She leaned in again, separating his lips with her tongue. She licked his bottom lip and tugged on it gently with her teeth. Max kissed her and let out a deep groan. He grabbed her butt and pulled her closer as he squeezed each cheek.

Vic was way over her head in lust with him. *Should I go slow or just let him throw me down and have me right here on the friggin' floor?* Every inch of Vic's body was throbbing, and by the looks of Max, his was too. "Okay... I'm going to go crazy here in about three seconds. Shouldn't we leave?" Vic asked in a breathless, raspy voice.

Max exhaled loudly. "You're a wicked woman, Victoria Maria Alonso. We can do this dance for a while—it's kind of hot." He kissed her again and gave her a smack on the ass. "Let's go, babe," he said, as he led her out the door.

Vic locked her fingers around Max's tight six-pack as he drove his Harley through town. Even the vibration of the bike beneath her made her imagine sex with him. Her mind wandered off to the party she was planning. She made a mental note to mention it to him at dinner. *I should be ashamed for wanting to test him. But how else can I be sure I'm the only woman he's thinking of? This isn't just a casual thing for me. He could be the real deal. I have to know before I become too invested in him.*

Max pulled up and parked the bike in a diagonal spot near the front door of Morey's. They walked in, arm in arm, and grabbed a booth in the back, where it was quieter and there were no TVs blasting sports on the screens to distract them. Max sat close and put his arm around Vic as they paged through the menu.

"Do you know what you want?" she asked casually.

"What kind of question is *that?*"

"I was talking about dinner, you goof. I'm having the cod sandwich with waffle fries. The food is really good here, so I'd recommend anything on the menu. You can't go wrong at Morey's."

"You sound like an advertisement. Does Morey pay you to promote the restaurant?" The expression on Max's face and the twinkle in his eyes showed he enjoyed their banter.

"You're nuts." *Okay, it's time to nonchalantly bring up the party.* "Oh, by the way, I want to invite you to a party

I'm having at my house on August 23. I haven't hosted a party in years, so I'm way overdue. Besides, I'd like you to meet more of my friends." Vic talked nonstop, more out of nervousness than anything else. She dipped her waffle fries in the puddle of ketchup that covered a quarter of her plate as she described the menu she'd serve on that day. She swirled each fry in the red pool, trying to pick up as much ketchup as possible before jamming it into her mouth.

Max watched, an expression of amusement on his face. Her arms flew as she got more excited, and she could hear her own voice rising a few octaves. Finally, he laughed.

"What? Did I say something weird?" She caught her breath long enough to ask the question.

"No, it's just that you're very animated when you're on a roll, that's all."

"I'm friggin' Puerto Rican, for Pete's sake. What do you expect?"

He laughed again. "I expect to be surprised by you every time I see you. Not only are you gorgeous, but you're funny, too. I like that about you. You're going to keep me on my toes, aren't you?"

"Well, Max Cole, I guess you'll have to figure that one out on your own," she said, making sure to smile with her teeth showing.

Chapter Eleven

Sasha set the morning aside to make calls to a few real estate agencies in Tarrytown in search of a buyer's agent. She wanted to find one whose personality she could work with and who had a high level of commitment to the client. She didn't like the vibe she got from the first agency she called. The woman on the phone sounded distracted and rushed as though she had somewhere else to be. She didn't take any time to ask Sasha what she was looking for in a home or even what neighborhoods interested her. Sasha hung up and scratched that company off her list. There were three more to go. She poured another cup of coffee, gave it a stir, and sat back down at Tina's kitchen table. Redmond Brothers Realty on Locust Street was number two on her list.

"Hello, Redmond Brothers Realty, Josh Redmond speaking. How may I help you?"

He had a nice voice, which was a plus in her opinion. Sasha decided she'd take notes if they got past the introductions.

"Hello, Mr. Redmond. My name is Sasha Renaud, and

I'm fairly new in Tarrytown. I'm interested in looking at some homes. Does your company have a buyer's agent?"

"Well, first off, Mrs. Renaud, welcome to Tarrytown."

Sasha was impressed that he was taking the time to welcome her, but she had to correct him. "I'm sorry, I don't mean to interrupt, but it's Ms. Renaud. I'd rather we got started off without any mistakes. I'm looking to buy a home for myself. I'm single, so it's only me you would be dealing with. I'm looking to buy an older, traditional home in a nice neighborhood."

"That sounds great, Ms. Renaud. I'm sorry about the assumption. May I call you Sasha so we can be more casual?"

"Of course—that's fine," she responded, flicking invisible crumbs off the kitchen table.

"Well, back to your initial question: yes we do have a buyer's agent. That would be myself, Josh Redmond. This agency has been in my family for thirty years, so we're very familiar with the Tarrytown housing market. My brother Jake and I run the company. We have several agents that work with us part-time, too. Jake works with the sellers, and I work with the buyers. What I would like to suggest, Sasha, is to meet near our office and go over what you want, and don't want, in a home. There's no point in wasting your time showing you something that doesn't fit your personality and lifestyle. We always take our potential clients out to lunch as a way to welcome them to the neighborhood. That way, we're in a neutral environment with no pressure and no expectations. What do you say? I have today at twelve fifteen open if you would like to meet at Tony's Club downtown. You can tell me everything you're looking for in a home, and I can give you some recommendations. We'll start the ball rolling and find you just what you're looking for."

"Okay, I can do that," Sasha said, feeling hopeful. "I'll have on a yellow dress."

"Wonderful. I'll be watching for you at twelve fifteen. Bring your wish list. Tarrytown is a great place to live. We'll find you the house you want. I'll see you in a few hours. I'm looking forward to meeting you."

Sasha began writing down the things she was looking for in a house. She needed three bedrooms, two baths, and a backyard that would be perfect for entertaining. She wanted to live in an older neighborhood where there were a lot of trees. The house had to be original to the neighborhood, a bungalow or a craftsman style preferably.

The clock on the microwave read ten fifteen. If Mia was available, there just might be enough time to check out Aaron's house before she met up with Mr. Redmond.

***

As she ran, dripping wet, down the hallway, trying not to slip, Mia caught the phone on its last ring. She and Reggie had gone for a nice run earlier, and the morning was hot and sticky. A shower was in order before she sat down to send out her photography invoices. She held the towel around her body, hoping all her vital areas were covered. The blinds were open, and Mia would be visible to any passerby on the sidewalk. Luckily, the large towel covered her well. "Hi, Sasha, what's up?" she asked, walking back to the bathroom as she talked.

"Mia, hi, do you have anything urgent planned this morning?"

"Urgent? No why?"

"I'm sorry it's last minute, but will you call Aaron and ask if I can take a quick peek at his house? I'm meeting with a realtor at twelve fifteen, and if Aaron's house and neighborhood are like I've envisioned, then that's the area I want to see."

"Sure, no problem. I've got some paperwork to do, but that can wait. I'll call Aaron now and get right back to you. I have a key to his house, so I can pick you up and take you over there. Believe me, you'll fall in love with the neighborhood. It's like you're in a Currier and Ives print."

"Oh goody, that's what I pictured. We can be neighbors. How fun would that be?"

"To be honest, Sasha, I can't wait to sell my house and move in with Aaron. You'll understand what I mean as soon as you see his place. Okay, get ready. I'll call you back in ten minutes."

Sasha tossed her wish list in her purse and threw on shorts and a tank top. She sat at the bathroom vanity and braided her long black hair—the humidity did strange things to it otherwise. Mia called back and said she was on her way. Sasha went outside and waited on the porch for the familiar sound of Mia's Camaro to come up the street. That car couldn't be confused with anyone else's. The deep sound of the exhaust was as distinct as a person's voice.

"Hey, thanks so much for doing this. I really appreciate it. I want to have a vision in my head when I explain to Mr. Redmond what I'm looking for." Sasha climbed in the passenger seat. "Ouch! Son of a bitch—this seat is hot. I think I just burned the back of my legs off."

"Sorry, hon, the seats are black leather, and it's ninety degrees outside. So, you're meeting with one of the Redmond brothers?" Mia smirked as she backed out of the driveway.

"Yeah, why—is there something wrong with them?"

"Which one are you meeting with?"

"Josh. I guess he takes care of the buyers, and his brother Jake takes care of the sellers."

"Oh, he'll take good care of you—I guarantee it," Mia said with a chuckle.

"What the hell does that mean?"

"Okay, I'll stop toying with you since you haven't lived here long enough to know the stories. I'll give you a quick rundown of the Redmond brothers of Tarrytown. Josh and Jake are twins. They're fraternal twins, so they don't look that much alike, but my God."

"My God, what?"

"Those boys are the Tarrytown tramps. Every woman in Westchester County that has a pulse has either had sex with one—or both—of them or wished she had."

"Oh… gross. That sounds too much like Jack. I'm going to cancel the appointment with him." Sasha felt thoroughly disgusted.

"No, go ahead and meet with him. It should be a real trip. They're both good at what they do. In real estate, I mean," Mia added, laughing. "You have to meet them, Sasha. They're both really gorgeous. Even if you don't hire Josh, you'll get a free lunch. Where are you meeting him?"

"At Tony's Club. Should I cancel?"

"No, just go. Take notice of all the women staring at you though. Tony's fills up at lunchtime. It should be a real kick to see how many girls are drooling and wishing they were in your shoes."

"Oh, for God's sake, Mia, how hot can he be?"

"Hotter than that seat you're sitting on. He's smokin' hot, sister... and I mean smokin' hot. Wavy blond hair with summer streaks in it, enormous brown eyes, dimples to die for, and a perfect tight ass. You get the picture." Mia turned onto Aaron's street. "Okay, enough about the Redmond boys. Pay attention now. Isn't this the prettiest street you've ever seen? Living on Oak Terrace Lane is like announcing you've arrived. This is one of the most beautiful streets in town. And check out the houses. If you want traditional, here it is, sister. There are cottages, craftsman style, Victorians, and awesome bungalows. Okay, here's Aaron's house. What do you think from the outside?"

"Oh my God—this is exactly like the image in my mind. It's like a storybook house."

"Isn't it? In my opinion, Aaron has one of the nicest houses in town—other than the big mansions that is. This home was his grandparents' place, then he bought it after they decided it was too much for them. They were so happy to keep this wonderful house in the family."

"I can see why. Look at that porch." Sasha gasped as she got out of the car. "It's huge and welcoming with the wicker chairs and table. Look at the ferns." Sasha was beside herself with excitement. "Do you think there are other houses this nice for sale in this neighborhood?"

"Well, that's what Mr. Hot Stuff is going to find out for you if you decide to hire him. Tell him you want a house similar to the ones on Oak Terrace Lane. He'll know what you mean." Mia unzipped the side pocket of her purse and pulled out Aaron's house key. "C'mon. Let's go inside."

"Why don't you have Aaron's key on your key ring?"

"I will eventually. I'm going to wait until I actually live here. Then the house will feel like mine, too. Right now, I'm a very privileged visitor. Hold your breath, Sasha— you're going to love this place."

Mia pointed out the original hardwood floors and elegant crown moldings. Even the hanging light fixtures were period pieces. The banister and newel post to the second floor were made of hand-carved walnut.

"Come outside and see the backyard—it's gorgeous." Mia led Sasha back down the stairs and through the kitchen to the beautiful red brick patio in the back. "This is the primo place to have a party. You can do something like this too as long as you find a house with big trees. A deck or patio off the kitchen would be perfect for entertaining." They sat for a while, each enjoying a Diet

Coke. Ancient oaks shaded the entire yard, cooling everything down. Finally, Mia said, "Well, it's almost noon. Do you want me to drop you off at Tony's?"

They locked up Aaron's house and walked down the driveway to her car.

"I guess you can drop me off," Sasha said. "It would be rude to cancel at the last minute, right? Crap, I told Mr. Redmond I'd be wearing a yellow dress. I wasn't thinking when I threw on shorts and a tank top."

"Who cares? You'll get there early so you can sit and watch. Believe me, that player will be hitting on the ladies, at least until he thinks it's time for you to walk through the door."

"How will I recognize him?" Sasha asked.

"Hang on." Mia spun the car around and turned left on Locust Street. She pulled up to the building where Redmond Brothers Realty was located. "There, on the window."

Mia pointed out an advertisement showing a picture of both brothers. "The one on the right is Josh," she said with a chuckle, waiting for Sasha's reaction.

"Holy shit! Thank God they aren't identical twins. Who could handle two of anything that gorgeous? But they're both perfect."

"Ya think? I told you so. Does Josh know you're single?"

"Well… yeah I told him because he called me Mrs. Renaud."

Mia cracked up. "Girl… with your beautiful face and his ego, all I can say is, look out."

Chapter Twelve

Mia dropped Sasha off near the front door of Tony's Club. "He's already here—probably prowling for his next conquest. See that gray Infinity across the street? That's his car. Good luck. Don't get sucked into his charm, and keep your legs crossed. Those shorts are pretty skimpy. Call me once you peel him off of you."

"Eww—that's so wrong, Mia!"

Mia laughed and gave a thumbs-up as she pounded her car through the gears and barreled away down Main Street.

Sasha walked into Tony's. She had never been there before and didn't know the layout of the place. She crossed through the old, squeaky doors to find a darkened—but rather upscale—bar area. It was nothing like the way she'd pictured it. The bar was horseshoe shaped with about thirty bar stools cozied up to the rail. It reminded her of an old-school, Frank Sinatra type of supper club, like a hidden treasure you might come across on a side street in Manhattan. The dining area was to her right, a little brighter and decorated nicely. Sasha claimed the only vacant bar stool. Tony's appeared to be the happening place for the lunch crowd. She sat, rearranged her shorts, and scanned the bar. She wanted to see if Mia's assessment of Josh was accurate. He might be a decent guy, sitting alone somewhere, going over the current listings he wanted to show Sasha. In the far corner of the bar, in the darkest area, she saw him. She had to take off her sunglasses just to make sure. There, sandwiched between two barely legal young ladies, was Josh Redmond. He was flirting shamelessly, and the women were eating it up. Each was trying to outdo the other with her wit and charm. All he had to do was stand between them and laugh at the appropriate times.

Hmmm… he is pretty gorgeous, but Mia was right. He's not even preparing for my arrival. Sasha looked at her watch—it was 12:02 p.m. *I guess as long as he can see the entrance and watch for a woman walking in wearing a yellow dress, he's got his ass covered. He can act like he just got here himself. What a jerk!*

She adjusted her shorts again, pulling them down a bit, then ordered a glass of sparkling water. "May I have a lime with that, please?" she asked as the bartender popped the bottle top and poured the Perrier into a rocks glass. Sasha nonchalantly turned her head to take another peek and was startled to find Josh standing right next to her. She jumped. He laughed.

"Hi, gorgeous. Sorry, I didn't mean to scare you. Am I that hard on the eyes?" He was fishing for a compliment, which Sasha had no intention of handing out.

"I'm waiting for someone," she replied coolly. She took a long, deliberate sip of her Perrier.

"I don't think we've met. I'm sure I'd notice someone as beautiful as you if I'd seen you here before. My name is Josh Redmond. I own one of the real estate agencies in town. So, hot stuff, what's your pleasure? Let me buy you a drink."

"No thank you, I have one." Sasha played it very cool as she turned away and looked in a different direction.

"Let me give you my business card. You can call me any time, day or night, if you want someone to show you the ropes."

"The ropes? What does that mean?" she asked dryly.

"Well, if you have to ask…" he said with a laugh. "I meant, if you want to get to know me, I'm well known around town. People like hanging out with me, plus I have connections."

"You mean the women like hanging out with you? Why do you think I'd want to get to know you anyway? I've got plenty of friends. What kind of connections do you have that I would need, Mr. Redmond?"

Sasha enjoyed taking his ego down a few notches. He clearly wasn't used to being on the defensive side of any conversation. She put Josh in his place, which was something that probably didn't happen to him often. He fumbled with his words.

"Okay then. Oops, I've got to go. I have an appointment in a few minutes. Nice talking to you, but I didn't get your name," he said, deflated.

"I didn't give it." Sasha took another sip of Perrier and watched as he turned and walked away. She glanced at her watch again. It was 12:18. *I'll make him wait for a few more minutes. He needs to squirm a little.* At 12:25, Sasha rose from the bar stool and walked toward Josh. His eyes lit up. *He probably thinks I've reconsidered. I'm sure he assumes a man like him is hard to resist.*

"Well... hi again, beautiful. Looks like your friend didn't show up, huh?" He looked Sasha up and down.

"Oh, he's here. Actually he's right in front of me."

Josh turned around, but nobody was standing there. "Sorry, babe, you've lost me."

"No, you've lost me. I'm out of here."

"Wait. What's your deal anyway? Having a bad day?" he asked with a snicker.

"Really? How dare you! Aren't you Josh Redmond from Redmond Brothers Realty? The Josh Redmond I'm supposed to meet here at Tony's? The alleged professional realtor that offered to treat me to lunch as he goes over homes he wants to show me? Isn't that you?" Sasha cocked her head as if she was totally bewildered.

"Son of a...! I thought you were going to wear a yellow dress. Sandra Renade, right?" he asked, sounding exasperated.

"Excuse me? Not *even* close, and why does it matter what I'm wearing? What does that have to do with your so-called professional courtesy? You're disgusting. I'll look for another realtor to work with. I've lost my appetite anyway." Sasha headed for the exit.

Josh threw a twenty on the bar and ran after her as she walked out the door. "Wait—I'm sorry. I'm at a loss for words here."

"Well, that's a plus," she sniped back.

"Not only are you beautiful, you're feisty, too. I like that," he said, grinning.

Her heart fluttered for a split second. "There you go again—so unprofessional. How in the hell do any clients take you seriously?" She stormed down the sidewalk. *Where the hell am I going? I have to look like I'm heading somewhere, damn it. I'll head toward the salon.*

"Please, sit down, and let me start over."

Sasha stopped and realized they were at the town square. Several vacant park benches were directly in front of her. Josh apprehensively reached for her arm.

"Please, I have so many wonderful homes to show you on paper. If you don't have any interest in them, you can write me off as a total loser and find some other buyer's agent to work with. Give me thirty minutes of your time, and if you don't mind, tell me your name again. I'd still like to buy you lunch." This time, the smile on Josh Redmond's face looked genuine.

Sasha took a deep breath, gathered her thoughts, and agreed to give him ten minutes of her time. If he didn't have a decent portfolio of homes to show her on paper, she would leave Josh Redmond and his ego in the dust.

"Let's go across the street to Amelia's. At least we can sit where it's air-conditioned. Let me buy you something like a burger and iced tea while I show you the listings I put together. If you have any interest, I might be able to show you a few today. Several of them are empty."

Sasha softened a bit out of nothing more than curiosity. She really wanted to see the vacant houses if they matched the style and location she was looking for. At this point, she thought of Josh Redmond as nothing more than a slimy snail groping for a sale.

***

They walked together across the street to Amelia's. The cool air took Sasha's breath away when they entered. Goose bumps rose on her arms from the extreme temperature change, and it didn't help that she was only wearing tiny shorts and a tank top.

"Here, let me give you my sports jacket to wear," he said, trying to break the ice.

A snide comeback was on the tip of her tongue, but Sasha accepted the jacket because she was freezing.

"May I please start over?" Josh opened his briefcase and pulled out the notes he'd scratched on a yellow legal pad earlier when he spoke with Sasha on the phone. He also had five folders filled with color photos and details about the houses he wanted to show her. *Yellow legal pad, yellow dress, wrong name—wow, I'm batting a whopping zero right now.* He casually glanced down and saw the name Sasha Renaud. Single woman, traditional houses, nice neighborhood. It all came back to him now. "Sasha, let me buy you something to eat and drink. Please—it's the least I can do. I really was a jag earlier—I'll be the first to admit that. Let me make it up to you. I promise I'll work hard at finding you a house to fall in love with."

***

A house I can fall in love with. That's exactly what I want. Sasha liked the way Josh described her house needs and finally agreed to let him buy her a chicken wrap and a club soda.

Josh grinned, exposing those deep dimples, and walked up to the counter to place their orders. She watched him. She wasn't about to fall for any man's sneaky tactics again. *I will admit, though, now that he's out of his element of being the pickup artist, he isn't that bad.*

They went over the five home portfolios Josh had brought along, and Sasha eliminated two of them right away. They just didn't do it for her. The other three were nice enough that she wanted to do a walk-through of each one.

"Okay, the houses on Richwood Drive and Woodland Place are vacant. We can head over there as soon as you're ready. The other one, we'll have to set up an appointment for. As far as homes similar to the ones on Oak Terrace Lane, I have to tell you, they're a bit pricey. There are three for sale in that general neighborhood though."

"What do you consider pricey?"

"Well, let me pull them up on my tablet and show you what I mean." Josh showed Sasha two of the three homes, which ranged in asking price from $675,000 to $907,000. The most expensive home didn't have a photo with the listing. The pictures looked nice, but the least expensive house had such a tiny backyard there would be no chance of even building a deck on the back. She eliminated that one from her wish list. They set up Saturday as the day to look at the two houses near Aaron's house and any others Josh could find that fit into Sasha's parameters. "Okay. If you're ready, let's check out the first two empty houses in today's listings." Josh paid the bill and led Sasha to his car.

They did a walk-through of the two houses. One was a maybe, and the other was very ordinary for the price. Sasha took detailed notes as Josh explained the pros and cons of each house. *He actually is good at being a realtor. Now, if he could only fall out of love with himself, he just might become a decent guy.*

Chapter Thirteen

Josh dropped Sasha off at the salon after they finished looking at the houses. She didn't want him taking her to Tina's house and asking a lot of questions. For all Sasha knew, Josh was acquainted with Tina. It seemed as though he was friends with all the single women in town. For the moment, the less information he had about Sasha, the better she liked it. She hadn't formed an opinion of him yet, either good or bad. Her focus was on buying the house of her dreams. She wanted a house to fall in love with.

Sasha bounded through the double doors of Hair Brained. The bell tower of the church two blocks away rang out three o'clock.

"Why does that gray car you got out of look like Josh Redmond's Infinity?" Vic asked with her nose scrunched up.

"Seriously, you guys, what's up with the Josh Redmond bashing?"

"Oh no—he got to you, didn't he?" Vic turned and winked at Tina, who was positioning Mrs. Edwards under the hairdryer. "Sasha, I'm not bashing him. Actually, I wouldn't mind a little piece of him myself, but he does have a serious reputation with the women in town. I'm just saying…"

"So I've heard. Anyway, he's my realtor. That is, unless he goes all bullshit ego on me again. How gross! I had to take him down a few notches. It was kind of cool to watch him squirm. I told him I would hire a different agent if he didn't start acting more professional."

"How did he take that?" Vic asked with a hearty laugh.

"He behaved after that. That guy is on a long-haul ego trip though. Is his brother like that too?" Sasha plopped down on an empty styling chair as Vic came over to examine the ends of her hair. Vic unbraided Sasha's dark mass of humid frizz and began a thorough search.

"Oh yeah—the Redmond brothers are Tarrytown's tramps in my opinion. You might need a serious body scrub after going out with one of them."

"How gross. I get the picture though. Thanks, Vic. Anyway, if you guys are free on Saturday, I'd love it if you'd tag along to look at houses. Josh is showing me at least three of them. I was pretty specific with the type of home I'm interested in and where I want to live. There's a couple in my price range within a few blocks of Aaron's house."

"No shit? You can afford that kind of house? When is the closing on your apartment?"

"It's in three weeks, but I can put earnest money down on a house if I find something I like. I mean, wouldn't that be cool to live in Aaron's neighborhood? Soon enough, Mia will live there, too."

"Do you have the 411 on something we don't?" Tina walked over and grabbed a handful of Sasha's hair. She joined in on the examination, her small scissors at the ready.

"Well, someday she and Aaron will get married. I'm just saying… that's all. Anyway, will you guys come? I'm going to call Karen, too, since she has a great eye for houses."

"I'm free," Vic said.

"Me too," Tina added. "You and I can drive over to Raunchy Redmond's office together in my car."

"You two are so immature." Sasha gave them a snooty expression and huffed. "Are you finding any split ends?" she asked, hoping they'd say no.

"Nope," Vic assured her. "And as a reminder, nobody better have anything planned for next Saturday, the twenty-third. That's the day of my party. Whoever is a no-show will answer to me. I'm going to have two lists: a list for lucky souls and a shit list for the people that better have a damn good excuse. Consider yourself warned."

Sasha looked toward Tina for safety. Tina rolled her eyes and laughed. "Don't worry, Vic. We actually want to live a long life. We'll be there. Anyway, we need to help you get the party ready."

***

Vic sat in bed with a notepad and pen that night. She listened as the much-needed rain pattered against her bedroom window. The sound soothed her. She was putting together the menu for her party and trying to come up with a theme. The party in honor of Aaron and Mia becoming a couple didn't really warrant a theme, but Vic did want something special for them. She decided on a cake with their pictures on it. Balloons and streamers would decorate the backyard. Vic's mind wandered off as she took a sip of the wine she brought into the bedroom. She thought about the real reason for the party. A certain part of her felt ashamed to be testing Max, but the other part needed the truth. She imagined how Max might act around Mia. *Will he long for her when he sees her or act like a casual friend? Will there be a twinkle in his eye when he glances her way? Why the hell am I tormenting myself like this? I hope Max is really as interested in me as he seems. If he's still fawning over Mia, then I guess we're done. I wonder if Aaron knows Max and Mia are acquainted with each other.* She was sure Max and Mia hadn't seen each other since the day Vic had met him. *That's been more than a month.* She drank the last gulp of wine to finish off the glass then punched her pillow into the shape she liked for sleeping. *It will be what it will be.* She switched off the lamp on the nightstand and fell asleep.

***

Saturday morning's breakfast was interrupted by the ringing doorbell. Tina and Sasha were just finishing their French toast. They laughed and agreed it had to be Karen. Tina yelled out for her to come in.

"Where are Mia and Vic?" Karen asked, looking at her watch. "We're supposed to be at Redmond Brothers Realty at ten o'clock. It's already nine thirty."

"Should I see if Mia wants to come? I didn't ask her," Sasha replied, now worried that she'd done the unthinkable.

"Well… duh. Of course, call her. Where's Vic?" Karen asked.

"She should be here any minute. I'll call Mia. Will I seem like a jerk doing this at the last minute?"

Karen and Tina grimaced at each other. "What do you think? We're not one through four. We're one through five, honey. Get used to it."

"Well, shit. Now I feel like an idiot."

"Just call her, and see if she wants to go along." Tina finished the last piece of French toast and stacked the plates in the dishwasher as Sasha took out her phone.

Mia picked up after a few rings. "Hello, Sasha. What's up?"

"Would you like to look at a few houses with us this morning? We'll be right in Aaron's neighborhood."

"Who's us?" Mia asked.

"Oh jeez, Mia—I'm so sorry. It's everyone except you. I didn't know if you and Aaron spent every weekend together, and—"

Mia laughed. "Take a breath, Sasha. Can Aaron come, too? Where should we meet you guys and Josh the slime ball?"

"Mia, seriously! Yes, Aaron can come, and the first

house is only two blocks from his place. The address is 640 Pineview. We'll be there in twenty minutes."

"That's a beautiful street with gorgeous homes. Any street within five blocks of Aaron's house would be similar to his. Maybe Josh knows how to do his job after all. See you in twenty. Out."

Sasha, Tina, Karen, and Vic waited in their cars in front of the real estate office. Josh pulled up, and an expression of disappointment crossed his face when he looked their way.

I bet he secretly hoped to have me all to himself today, Sasha thought.

"Hello again, Sasha. I see you have some friends tagging along. Tina, Vic, how's it going? I don't believe I've met this last young lady."

"My name is Karen, and I'm thirty-seven, but thanks for the compliment… I think."

"Okay, then. I'll lead the way. You can follow me to the first address."

"You guys actually know Josh Redmond?" Sasha asked once he walked away. She was surprised that he'd called Vic and Tina by name.

"Of course. You're going to have to adjust to living the small-town life. Tarrytown isn't Manhattan, and yes, everyone that has lived here for more than five years is well acquainted with everyone else."

"Oh, I like that idea already. I'm going to have *so* many friends soon." Sasha became excited just at the thought of it.

"Just remember, knowing everyone's business and everyone knowing yours is a double-edged sword. It will keep you honest—that's for sure. Okay, we're here. Just park behind Mr. Grossmond, Tina," Vic said, laughing.

Aaron and Mia were already waiting on the sidewalk in front of the house. They said their obligatory hellos to Josh. Aaron even shook his hand.

"It's amazing," Sasha said, realizing they were also acquainted with Josh. "It's simply amazing."

The houses were similar to Aaron's, so he knew which questions to ask. Sasha was grateful for his help. She took pictures with her cell phone and scribbled down notes as fast as Josh spoke the words. She had the listing papers, too, as backup. The first house was a large red brick bungalow. It had a front porch similar to Aaron's, but the backyard wasn't any bigger than the previous home she'd already eliminated. Sasha was ready to move on to the last house for sale in that part of town. This was the most expensive one, listed at $907,000, three blocks to the west on Sunrise Avenue. They pulled up to the curb and parked under a row of ancient oaks that lined the street.

Sasha let out a gasp when she saw the house. "No way—this can't be the right place!"

An enormous Victorian mansion, with gingerbread accents covering every inch of the facade, stood before her. It was situated on a double lot with hedges calling out the property lines instead of boring fences. It was big, bold, and worn out. It was in need of repair, and lots of it. The paint was peeling off the clapboard siding, and the roof looked to be in bad shape. The yard was a dense mass of foot-tall weeds. Those were just the obvious problems visible from the outside.

Sasha stood on the sidewalk, her mouth agape, as she took in every inch of the exterior. The group stared at her. Then she felt a huge smile erupt on her face, and she began to giggle. "You guys, it's happening. This is the house I'm going to fall in love with."

"What?" they all said at the same time.

"Hurry, Josh—I have to see the rest of it. Open the front door *pleeese!*"

"Sasha, take it down a notch," Aaron whispered in her ear. "Don't show how excited you are, or you'll end up paying full price."

"But Josh is a buyer's agent, Aaron," she said, still completely amped up.

"Right, but he gets paid commission based on the price the house sells for. Point out the negatives and how much it will cost to fix this place up. You can get it for a much lower price if you do. Ask how long it's been on the market. No matter how much you like the inside, stop acting excited about it."

"Okay, if you say so. I hope you know what you're talking about. Still, I can't wait to get through the door. Josh, how long has this house been for sale? And how long has it been vacant?" Sasha made sure to turn her nose up when they passed over the threshold. "Eww... this place smells like old people and mildew. What's *that* about?"

"Well, according to the listing description, the house

has been vacant for fourteen months. It probably just needs a good airing out and cleaning."

Sasha had a hard time suppressing her excitement. She was falling in love and falling fast. All the floors were original maple hardwood. The woodwork was ornate and intact throughout the house. Three working fireplaces adorned the library, dining room, and formal living room. Stained glass windows were everywhere. The house was huge, totaling thirty-seven hundred square feet in size. It included five bedrooms, three and a half baths, a library, parlor, formal living room, dining room, and a kitchen large enough to entertain in. The square footage didn't even include the attic and basement, which were gigantic. The inside needed updated electrical and plumbing, but other than that, only cosmetic work. Sasha visualized this diamond in the rough turning into a masterpiece. The dust and old-people smell didn't faze her. She just needed to act as if it did.

There wasn't a way to access the backyard from the kitchen, but the wall was long enough to put in a nice set of French doors. They followed the sidewalk to the back of the house, ending up in the oversized backyard. Sasha's imagination ran wild. There were enormous oaks and flowering trees. The hedges followed the property line, creating a beautiful natural border. All she needed to do was hire someone to trim things back to a reasonable state. She pictured a multileveled deck coming off the kitchen. Red brick pavers would lead to the flower gardens, and the deck would have wooden spindles for railings, matching the house. There was enough room in the backyard to have a gazebo and water feature. Sasha was over the moon, but thanks to Aaron's advice, she changed her attitude in front of Josh. She couldn't show her hand yet. She'd put an offer on the table but not until she went over things privately with Aaron.

"It has potential, but there's a ton of work to do. I'm not sure if I have enough ambition to take on a project quite this size. I'll have to run the numbers and get back to you, Josh. I'm sure the repairs and updates could get very expensive. Meanwhile, schedule at least three more houses for me to check out this week. I'm busy next weekend so don't set anything up then. Call me."

They said good-bye and watched as Josh drove away. As soon as his car rounded the corner, Sasha let out a squeal of delight and jumped up and down on the sidewalk.

"Seriously, I can do this. I know I can. This is the house I'm going to buy. Even if it costs a hundred thousand dollars to fix it up, I'm going to buy the Victorian. I'm already in love with it. Please, Aaron, can we go to your house and talk this over? I really need your advice. I wouldn't mind a glass of wine, either, to help calm me down."

Chapter Fourteen

Aaron and Mia walked back to his house. The girls piled into Karen's car and met them there. The group gathered around Aaron's kitchen table with the house listing in front of them, each babbling anxiously. On the cutting board, Mia sliced fruit and put together a pitcher of sangria while each person took turns offering their take on the house. Aaron poured Sasha a glass of Merlot to hold her over then told her to sit still and listen to what everyone had to say. Karen began and was in total agreement with Sasha. The house was magnificent. Tina was against it, rational woman that she was. The house was far more than Sasha needed, being only one person. Aaron thought it would be absolutely beautiful when completed, but the cost of repairs could sway him in either direction. Vic was for it as long as Sasha hosted most of the house parties from now on. They all looked at Mia, waiting for her to speak her peace.

"What? I'm giving this serious thought," she said with a devilish smile.

"C'mon, Mia, I need your opinion. We have one no,

two yeses, and Aaron's on the fence. What's it going to be?" Sasha asked.

"Are you out of your mind? Is this really the house you want with all the work you'd need to do?" Mia shook her head.

"Well… yes it is," Sasha said, standing her ground even though she could feel the pouty bottom lip coming out.

Mia finally grinned and said, "That's my girl. You're damn right this is the house for you, and we're all going to help you remodel it. But we do need to find out what the costs will be first. You can reduce your offer substantially based on the work it needs, and how long it's been on the market. Tomorrow, we're going to make the calls and have a few contractors give you estimates. Of course, Josh has to meet us there, but you can still act like you haven't decided on anything yet. Keep him guessing by viewing other houses until we have a firm price in mind to offer."

Sasha bounced around the table, hugging everyone. She was overjoyed at the idea of making the Victorian her very own. If she could recreate the vision in her mind, this worn-out Victorian house could turn into a stunning home.

"Karen, you should sell your house and move in there with me. It's plenty big. Pretty soon, we'll all be living within five minutes of each other. How great is that?"

"That's pretty great, Sasha. It really is," Mia said with a wink in Aaron's direction.

***

Tuesday afternoon, Sasha and Mia were again standing on the maple-floored foyer of the Victorian. Josh, Bob Anderson—the plumber—and Frank Diaz, the electrician, met them there. The contractors went from room to room, checking every water pipe and electrical wire. They told Sasha the estimates might take a few hours to put together. Josh followed Mia and Sasha around like a lost puppy. Sasha made a point of never being alone, to keep him from trying to ask her out.

"Josh, don't you have something to do like call clients?" Mia asked, sounding irritated.

Sasha and Mia had plenty of ideas to talk about alone as they walked. Sasha didn't want to give Josh any indication yet of how interested she was until she got the numbers from the contractors.

"Yeah… I guess I can wait in my car," Josh replied, somewhat deflated.

Two hours went by while the girls planned the colors schemes for each room. They'd agreed on the way that the deck should be designed for the best traffic flow coming off the kitchen. Mia scratched out diagrams as Sasha picked areas in the backyard to start flower beds and the perfect spot for the future gazebo and water feature. The contractors left after handing Sasha the estimates. The girls followed them outside, said good-bye, and noticed that Josh was sound asleep in the driver's seat of his car.

"Josh!" Sasha yelled, trying to startle him. He jumped, and they laughed. "I've got the estimates from the contractors, so we're going to take off. I figured you would want to lock up before you left. Call me Thursday and tell me where to meet you. We still have a few houses to view this week, right?" She tucked the estimates safely in her purse.

"Yeah, we sure do," he said, rubbing the sleep out of his eyes. "I'll call you Thursday morning. See ya."

"Bye," the girls said together and left.

Mia and Sasha drove to Hair Brained. They found Vic and Tina on the patio behind the salon, taking a break. They huddled in a group to review the estimates.

"Hang on—I've got to tell Jennifer where we are in case anyone needs us." Vic left and returned a few minutes later, carrying two small four-packs of Merlot and plastic cups.

"Okay, the electricity update will run $27,478," Sasha said. "That includes outdoor lighting and the garage, too. The plumbing estimate is $44,916. What does that total, Mia?"

Mia opened the calculator icon on her phone. "Hold on, it's um… $72,394 for everything."

"Okay, you guys," Vic said. "The house has been vacant for friggin' ever, and it stinks like hell. Sure, it's on a double lot, which is a bonus, but it isn't like you're going to sell that to someone to build on. You wouldn't want another house up in your grill. So, the fact that it's on a large lot is nice, but not necessarily beneficial to you. They're asking $907,000, right?"

"That's right," Sasha said. "What's a fair price in your opinion? I'm going to run it past Aaron, too, but give me your take."

"I'd offer $775,000 and not a damn penny more," Vic said. "That price would take the total investment with repairs to around $850,000, give or take. Mia, run the exact numbers quick."

"Okay… it's $847,394. Close enough."

"That's a fair price, Sasha," Tina said. "Anyone else would offer $50,000 less right out of the gate, and don't forget how long it's been for sale. The owners must be desperate by now. Start out low with a crackhead offer, and see how it goes. You can always negotiate. Shit… hold everything—we totally forgot about the roof and exterior paint."

Sasha pressed her temples. "I'm getting a friggin' headache. How much would the outside repairs add to the cost?"

"Probably fifty grand," Mia said. "Here's what I'd do. I'd offer $700,000, and see if they bite. Like Tina said, you can always negotiate. Remember, the owners live somewhere else, the house isn't bringing in rental income, and they're stuck paying the utilities and property tax. I bet they'd be stoked to get that monkey off their back. C'mon, Sasha. Let's go over to the camera store and see what Aaron thinks. Later, guys."

"Adios, and good luck. Keep us posted."

Aaron listened to Mia's suggestion and agreed that $700,000 was a good starting point, based on the appraisals and the work needed on the exterior. Several customers entered the shop, so Mia and Sasha left and walked to Bottoms Up.

"Mia, do you really think I can get this house? I'll admit it's going to be a huge project, but I can't stop daydreaming about it."

"That's a good sign, honey. Be realistic, but also be true to yourself. We know what the repairs will cost. Your apartment is going to close in a few weeks. It's just about a wash when you consider the selling price of your apartment and the price you'll pay for the house. Believe it or not, your insurance and property tax will be much lower here. Can you imagine how beautiful the house will be when it's fixed up?"

"That's all I've been doing. I've been dreaming about it and sketching out ideas. I haven't even bought it, yet I'm putting all this energy into it. I've found my future, and it's all because of you."

"That isn't true," Mia said. "If Jack hadn't cheated on me, we would never have met."

"That's right, but you're the one who rescued me from him. You could have divorced Jack and been done with it. I wouldn't have known he was ever married. You got in the middle of it, maybe with different intentions originally, but look how it's changed me. I was a self-indulgent spoiled brat when we met. I'm so grateful now. I love you and this town. I love the girls and Aaron. I'm happy now. I have friends, and that's saying a lot for me. Who would have ever thought my life would do such a turn around? I'm so blessed." Sasha's eyes teared up, and she hugged Mia. "We're like sisters, right?"

"Yes, Sasha—we're like sisters."

Chapter Fifteen

After looking at several more properties that week, Sasha hadn't changed her mind about the Victorian. She wanted to do the responsible thing and compare properties, but nothing could come close to the house on Sunrise Avenue. She liked that street name. It sounded happy and optimistic. A thought entered Sasha's mind as she spoke the name Sunrise Avenue out loud. *I'll have a balcony built off the second-floor master suite. It faces east, so I can watch the sun rise every morning.* That idea in itself was an epiphany. The house was destined to be hers.

Sasha asked Mia to join her at Redmond Brothers Realty Thursday morning. Dragging it out any longer would be futile. She would submit an offer that day. She'd start with a low first offer and go from there. At ten o'clock, Sasha and Mia sat in Josh's office, ready to present the initial offer. Sasha told Josh the number she had in mind and reached for the contract he was holding.

"Are you serious right now, Sasha? I can't present such a low offer to the owners. It's an insult." Josh snickered and snatched the contract back before it was in her hand.

The last six weeks had changed Sasha considerably. She had grown into a confident woman and wasn't about to stand for Josh's attitude. She resembled a mother bear protecting her cub. That house was going to be hers, come hell or high water.

"Do I need to remind you, Mr. Redmond, who you work for?" Sasha stood and leaned across his desk. The niceties blew out the window and she reverted back to formality. Josh would end up on the burn pile in a heartbeat if he didn't watch himself. He had to submit the offer if he ever hoped to have Sasha speak to him again.

"Fine, but you're going to alienate yourself from them."

"Just friggin' do it, Josh! I'll be waiting to hear from you tomorrow. Give me that contract to sign. Make sure you tell the owners there aren't any contingencies to worry about. It's going to be a cash transaction in two weeks. That should pique their interest. Now, where do I sign?"

***

Eighteen people were on Vic's guest list for Saturday. In addition to her usual best friends, she expected a few people from Morey's and Scott from Bottoms Up. Six cousins from the Bronx planned to come, but the person Vic was most excited about showing off was her brother Mario. They hadn't seen each other in four years. He'd just moved back to New York after running a successful shop in Telluride, Colorado for the last few years. Mario's business began as a ski school initially, but quickly expanded to sell everything related to skiing. He soon bought the space next to his store and enlarged it to include summer sporting equipment. It did so well that Mario decided to open another ski school and store in Hunter, New York. Hunter was a great choice, being in the northern Catskill Mountain region with plenty of summer and winter outdoor activities to participate in. Being less than two hours from Tarrytown, where he'd grown up, was an extra bonus.

Mario had promised to attend the party and said he was excited to spend the week in Tarrytown visiting old friends and his crazy sister. Vic was anxious to introduce her brother to Max since they had very similar interests.

Still, the reason for the party was twofold. Of course, Mia—being Vic's dearest friend—deserved a party thrown in her honor. She was way overdue for happiness, and Aaron was the best guy in the world to share that happiness with. But Vic had to see for herself what Max's expression and demeanor would be like again around Mia. If nothing seemed amiss, she would let her insecurities go and move on blissfully with Max.

***

The man wearing a Yankees baseball cap and sunglasses swung the salon door open and sauntered in at ten o'clock. Vic and Tina glanced up from their work for a split second then continued the latest gossip without missing a beat. Jennifer, the receptionist, took care of the walk-ins. The stranger approached the counter and asked for Victoria

Alonso. Jennifer offered him a beverage and excused herself to get Vic.

"She'll be right with you, sir. Please have a seat." Jennifer handed the stranger a Diet Coke.

Vic gave him a quick once-over as she finished Ashley Nelson's comb out. He appeared somewhat unkempt with long dark hair pulled back in a ponytail. He wore several earrings in each earlobe and tan cargo shorts with Birkenstock sandals. The stranger seemed muscular under the tight T-shirt, just a little rough around the edges.

He needs a haircut and a shave, for sure, but how does he know me by name? Vic accompanied Ashley to the reception desk to have Jennifer set up her next appointment. She expressed her thanks with a generous hug and said good-bye. Vic turned and approached the man, who was sitting in the waiting area, paging through an *InStyle* magazine. He held his head low, his face obscured by the hat and sunglasses. "Hi. Is there something I can help you with? Jennifer said you asked for me personally."

He lifted his head and paused for a second. A huge smile broke out on his face. "Hey, Sis, what's up?"

"You son of a bitch!" Vic shrieked. She grabbed Mario and nearly squeezed the life out of him. "What the hell happened to the clean-cut brother I used to have? I thought you were a vagrant. And what's with the piercings? You're such a dork."

"C'mon—I don't look that bad, do I? Blame it on Colorado. I'm my own boss, so I can look however I want.

You've heard of that laid-back, outdoorsy lifestyle, haven't you, Vic?"

She knew it all too well. Max had the same demeanor, and she loved it. Vic had checked out Mario's photos on Facebook and spoken to him over the phone, but in person, it was much clearer that he had changed dramatically over the last four years. She had often thought about Mario, picturing him sitting at a large, mahogany desk counting stacks of money—not the image he projected now. He had the Colorado ski-town business-owner appearance that made him look like a ski bum himself. The only thing missing was a dog lying in the doorway of the shop that each customer would have to step over when they entered.

"I love the changes, Mario. You're going to do great in Hunter, too. I'm so happy for you and your success, and I'm glad you're home. There's someone I want you to meet tomorrow at the party. I'm sure you'll hit it off right away since he's a lot like the new you. His name is Max, and he was just talking about opening an outdoor sporting goods shop himself."

"Well, that sucks. Are we going to be competitors?" Mario asked.

"I don't think so, Bro. He's talking about a shop closer to this area. What if you guys came up with something together and had a few stores in New York? Max could run an outdoor-sports shop that focuses more on hiking, camping, and mountain biking. Since he's a wilderness guide, he could offer guided daily—or weekly—hiking trips, too. That's more the type of activities people do around here."

"You might be on to something, Sis. I'll pick his brain this next week to see if he's really serious about opening a store. He might be interested in having a partner—or maybe not. Anyway, besides stopping in to say hi and telling you I've arrived, I'd like to shower and grab a short nap. Can I have the house keys? I'll come back in a few hours and take you out for lunch. How does that sound?"

"It sounds awesome. I'll see you at noon." Vic handed him the keys and blew a kiss in his direction. She shook her head and chuckled at the sight of the curly black ponytail that reached the middle of her younger brother's back. With her hands firmly planted on her hips, she watched him out the salon window. Mario walked toward his car without a care in the world. He climbed into an orange Karmann Ghia convertible and drove away. Vic, still grinning, picked up her cell phone and called Mia and Karen.

They agreed to meet at Bottoms Up at twelve fifteen. They had to go over the plans for Saturday's party anyway. Vic decided to surprise Mia with Mario's presence. Mia knew he'd be attending the party, but she had no idea he'd arrived a day early. Karen had never met him, so she wouldn't be thrown with his altered appearance.

They sat on the red brick patio behind Bottoms Up. The new patio was a much-needed addition to the seating area, especially with the tourists swarming Tarrytown as they did every summer. Mario, Vic, and Tina watched for

Mia as they laughed and caught up with each other's shenanigans over the past four years. They all turned when Mia and Karen walked in.

"No friggin' way!" Mia ran toward Mario and landed a strong punch to his shoulder before embracing him and giving him a wet kiss on the cheek. "What the hell is this shit you've got going on, Mario?" she asked while pulling on his ponytail and trying to make the introductions between Karen and him.

***

The girls chattered like barnyard hens as they summarized Mario's life in a nutshell. Karen saw the family resemblance between Vic and Mario. The dark curly hair, enormous hazel eyes, and olive skin gave away the Puerto Rican ethnicity they shared as brother and sister. He had a hot, wild, edgy appearance that Karen realized was strangely appealing to her. She'd always thought of herself as more proper, never veering much to the left or right of the typical ho-hum male she dated in the past. A monotone, predictable guy was easier to deal with than someone all the girls were attracted to. In college, it was the nerdy, but slightly attractive, techie guys. Ordinary seemed safer. A few years later, it was Jack the jerk— arrogant but successful as a clean-cut sales manager. Karen didn't date after divorcing Jack. Men in general had been more irritating than interesting until now. She secretly took her own pulse as the five of them sat on the patio of Bottoms Up, enjoying their lunch.

Chapter Sixteen

Luckily, the cloud cover broke Saturday morning and made way for a gloriously sunny day. The weather gods were smart not to ruin Vic's party. There would be hell to pay otherwise. She was in good spirits because of Mario but a little anxious about Mia and Max. *Whatever... it will all be fine. It has to be. Mia is with Aaron, and she wouldn't risk losing that for someone she slept with once... or twice.* Vic tried to erase those negative thoughts as she poured pancake batter on the hot griddle. The scent of bacon frying took her back to her childhood. Saturdays were meant for watching cartoons, playing jump rope on the sidewalk, and fighting with her siblings. The Alonso family, being typical Bronx, New Yorkers with four kids, worked hard to support and raise them right. Saturday was the bonus day of the week when everyone was at home having pancakes and bacon for breakfast. Sunday mornings were spent at St. Boniface Catholic Church until eleven, with the kids squirming restlessly in the pews. They were often on the receiving end of threatening looks from their larger-than-life father.

"Breakfast is ready!" Vic called out to Mario, who was sleeping in the guest bedroom three doors down the hall on the right.

***

He woke to the sound of a voice coming from the kitchen. Mario rolled over, rubbed his sleep-caked eyes, and looked around. The room was unfamiliar. He stretched, yawned to increase the oxygen flow to his brain, and remembered. *Oh yeah—I'm at Vic's.* In just three days, he'd driven from Telluride to Hunter and then on to Tarrytown with very little sleep. Mario inhaled the scents of fresh coffee brewing and maple-flavored bacon frying. There was a direct path from the kitchen to the hallway, then under his door where the aroma found an entrance and wafted through his room. It was wonderful, and he realized now how he missed having a woman in his life. Of course, Vic was there, and she could cook, but having someone to love again was another story. He thought briefly about Sarah as he dressed. *What is she doing now that I'm gone? Does she have any regrets, or is she happy with Brad, the bastard?* She was the real reason Mario had left Colorado. Cheating was one thing, but with Brad, his best friend and head ski instructor? The pain and betrayal were too great for him to remain in Telluride. Mario fired them both and hired several new people to oversee the ski school and run the store.

"Mario, your breakfast is going to get cold," Vic yelled out. Her voice snapped him back into reality.

"Okay, I'm coming, gotta put some clothes on first." He was happy to be in Tarrytown again. He'd met Karen yesterday, and there would be more new faces today. He was looking forward to meeting Max at the party. Mario wanted to stay busy, and what better way than to have several stores going? It would help keep his mind off Sarah. Plus Max sounded like exactly the type of person Mario wanted as a business partner.

He planted a huge kiss on Vic's cheek as he danced his way into the kitchen. Lively Spanish music played throughout the house. She laughed at his antics and danced along with him.

"I love you, Bro. Now, sit your ass down and eat before I have to throw everything into the microwave," she said, waving a bubblegum-pink-polished fingernail at him.

"Damn, woman—you're just like Mom," he teased.

"You've got that right. You better be afraid, my pretty—very afraid!" she said with a laugh.

"So, what's the story with Karen?" he asked between mouthfuls of pancakes.

"Are you interested? I wouldn't have pictured her as your type. That whole hippy-dippy, mountain-man thing you've got going on gives a different vibe. I'm surprised you didn't scare her off yesterday."

"Hey, I saw how she looked at me."

"Really? And how was that, hot shot?"

"I don't know. She just looked… intrigued… I guess."

"You dumbshit. I was intrigued when you came into the salon. Who wouldn't be curious when a wild-looking, long-haired, pierced dude strolls into Tarrytown? Heaven forbid it turned out to be my own brother, for crap's sake. Want some more pancakes?"

"Hell yeah. I have to admit, Vic, you're a damn good cook."

"Well, Bro, you're going to man the grill today. I'm just saying. And after we eat this afternoon, I think you and Max should get acquainted and run some ideas by each other."

"For sure, that's the plan. I'll take some more bacon if there's any left," he said while licking his fingers clean.

***

The backyard began to take shape. With Mario's help, it started to look more like Party Central than a typical residential backyard in Tarrytown. Mario reminisced about the many family parties years ago with their crazy cousins.

"Do we have enough beer and wine?" he asked, knowing how much they liked to drink. He wrapped streamers around the trunks of several small trees and hung lights from the oaks near the patio while Vic checked the beverage supply.

"We have ten cases of beer and twenty-five bottles of wine. I hope we'll talk and eat, too. I don't want eighteen people camped out on my living room floor tonight because they're all wasted. Could you imagine?" Vic giggled, remembering the cousins.

The sound of car doors slamming and people laughing

echoed from the front of the house.

"Mario, go around through the side gate and lead people back here. By the sound of things, it has to be the cousins out front."

He laughed and disappeared around the house. Within minutes, there were six Puerto Ricans kissing Mario, pinching his cheeks, and yelling at the top of their lungs in Spanish. They hugged Vic so tightly she was sure a few ribs cracked. A mountain of food was dumped on the picnic tables. The ringing doorbell and humming of Vic's cell phone sounded at the same time.

"Mario, get the door. It has to be Karen. She's the only person I know that rings a doorbell. I've got a call coming in." Vic found a quiet spot near the garage to talk. Hearing anything over the voices of excited Puerto Ricans was next to impossible. "Hello," she said, knowing full well who was on the other end.

"Hey, babe, it's Max. I'm on my way. I should be there in about thirty minutes. Is there anything you need other than me?"

"No, you'll do just fine. Seriously, I could never run out of anything now that my cousins have arrived. I'm sure Scott and Morey's clan are bringing things, too, but thanks for asking. I can't wait to see you. I've missed you, Max."

"That's nice to hear. I've missed you too. Sounds like the party is already off to a good start. I'll see you in a few. Bye."

"Bye." Vic felt giddy every time she spoke to him. Max

would be easy to love. If he actually started an outdoor-sports business with Mario, everything would fall into place just as it should. The possibilities excited her.

Vic returned to the backyard to find more people had arrived, including Mia, Aaron, Tina, and Sasha. Her best friends were all there, everyone she loved the most except Max. He would arrive soon. *Do I really love him?* Today might be her turning point. She would see for herself how he reacted to Mia.

Bottles of wine flowed among the ladies. The guys helped themselves to an abundance of beer in coolers strategically placed throughout the yard. Gossip, stories, and loud music filled the air. Dancing Puerto Ricans entertained the crowd. The neighbors gathered, inviting themselves because they knew a better time would be had at Vic's house than at their own. Vic paid close attention to Mia and Aaron's body language. It was obvious they were in love.

Why the hell am I so insecure? Vic excused herself to go inside, saying she was getting more snacks. She needed some quiet, if only for a few minutes, before Max showed up. She followed the air-conditioned hallway to the master bedroom, wiping her clammy forehead as she walked. The indoor temperature seemed comfortable and not at all humid, yet Vic felt overheated. *It's nerves—that's all. I just need to breathe deep and relax for a minute. I can talk myself out of this. I know I can,* she thought as the ringing in her ears and nausea overcame her. "Oh shit." It came up her throat without warning. Vic bolted for the bathroom and threw up in the sink. There wasn't enough time to even lift the toilet seat and vomit like a dignified woman. "Son of a bitch, what the hell is wrong with me? I friggin' need a shrink or some Xanax, damn it!" She wrapped a large wad of toilet tissue around her hand and scooped up as much vomit as possible, flushing it down the commode. Just the act of doing that almost sent her into another round of projectile vomiting.

She recognized the sound of Max's motorcycle pulling into the driveway. "Son of a bitch!" she wailed again. She launched herself into the bedroom and peeked out the window facing the driveway. Max pulled the bike back on its kickstand and headed for the front door. "Mother of God—I have puke breath, and he's ready to knock on the door," Vic cried out to the bedroom walls. She dove back into the bathroom and guzzled half a bottle of mouthwash, gargled, and spit it into the sink. *Rinse-repeat-rinse-repeat,* the voices in her head commanded. She wiped her face with a cool washcloth and ran down the hall to the foyer. He'd already knocked twice. She stopped, caught her breath, looked at herself in the foyer mirror to make sure she didn't have any residue on her teeth, and opened the door. There in her face, stood the man who sucked the air right out of her lungs. Max was the first-place Adonis of Westchester County with Aaron and Mario tying for second place.

"Hello, gorgeous!" he said as he took her in his arms. "I've missed you, and I'll admit I was pretty excited to get here." Max kissed her softly at first, but the passion increased as she responded.

I wonder how long I can hold my breath, Vic thought as she melted in his arms. Max didn't react negatively, so she assumed her breath was okay. "You want to go out back and mingle? My brother Mario got here yesterday, and he's anxious to meet you." She desperately wanted to have a drink of something, anything. *Alcohol has to smell better than vomit breath.*

"Sure—lead the way." Max squeezed her butt as they walked.

Vic giggled as she led him by the hand to the patio. They joined the group, and she introduced Max to her neighbors, a few cousins he hadn't met at the wedding, and Mario. Vic also introduced Max to Aaron. Before she had the chance to say he was Mia's boyfriend, Aaron stood up and shook Max's hand. As Aaron was about to introduce Max to Mia, Max grinned, stepped to the side, and embraced Mia. The awkward silence seemed to last forever before Aaron spoke up. "Oh, you've already met?"

"Yeah, we're old friends. Long time no see. How are you, Mia?" Max teased.

Mia stammered with her face flushing bright red. "I'm fine, thanks. Can I get anyone a refill?"

Aaron gave them each an odd look. "No thanks, honey, I think we all have full drinks. So, how are you two acquainted?" he persisted with a gulp of beer.

"I introduced them to each other several months ago. That was around the time Mia hurt her ankle," Vic quickly interjected. The relief in Mia's eyes was evident, and that lie became the new truth. Aaron accepted the explanation and began talking to Max about living in Tarrytown all his life.

Looking confused, Max was starting to speak up when Mario joined the conversation. Mario pulled Max aside and explained how he wanted to discuss business opportunities with him next week. The two seemed to hit it off, which was a huge relief to Vic.

As the hostess, she needed to mingle. *How the hell am I going to watch Max if I'm trying to keep everyone else entertained?* She solved the problem by getting her friends to help. Tina introduced Sasha to more people as they both helped to keep the food, conversation, and beverages flowing.

The tapping sound of the fork against a crystal wineglass got everyone's attention. One by one, they joined in until the ringing sound filled the backyard.

Vic stood, laughed, and silenced the crowd. She blew an air kiss to her best friend and began. She explained that although she didn't really need a reason to host a long-overdue party, this one did hold a special place in her heart. As Mario helped Vic unroll an enormous banner, she asked Aaron and Mia to stand. The banner read, "Congratulations, Mia and Aaron. It's about damn time." The crowd laughed and clapped as Vic explained that two of her dearest friends had finally got it right. Karen and Sasha appeared from the kitchen, carrying a large sheet cake to set on the picnic table. The images in the frosting were high school senior pictures of Aaron and Mia. Mario, who'd been close to Aaron when they were growing up, made a champagne toast to the newly outed couple.

Vic scanned the crowd for Max. He stood at the far backyard, leaning against an oak tree, staring at Mia. Vic's heart sank. It was obvious Max was blindsided about the party being in Aaron and Mia's honor. *Max, please, please, get over her,* Vic prayed. The joyful sounds of laughter faded into the background. The only thing Vic heard was the pounding in her temples. In that moment, she was sure love would never be hers. *I'm not as beautiful as Mia with her flawless figure and golden hair.* Vic couldn't stop staring at Max as he walked up to Mia. Mia turned to see who'd tapped her shoulder, and he whispered something in her ear. She smiled and nodded. They left together shortly afterward.

***

Max and Mia reconnected in the front yard where it was quiet enough to talk.

"I'm really happy for you and Aaron," Max said when they reached the driveway. "Follow me—I brought something for you." He led her over to the saddlebags of his Harley and pulled out a beautifully wrapped box. "The timing is weird, I'll admit."

"Why?" she asked as he handed the gift to her.

"I had no idea this party was for you and Aaron. This gift is just a small token to show how much I appreciate you. Mia… you're the only friend I've ever told my story to. You didn't judge me, either. Then what you said that day in the park really hit me. You told the truth—that you loved Aaron, and we didn't have a future together. You didn't lead me on or sugarcoat anything. It was painful to hear—I won't lie—but now I can move forward without wondering if we had a chance. You let me know where I stood, and I respect that. You let me down gracefully and didn't bruise my ego too much." He laughed. "Anyway, I'm in a good place, and I have you to thank. Vic is a wonderful woman. I'm hoping for a future with her. Okay… I guess I'm babbling too much. So, go ahead— open it. I wanted this moment to be private, just between you and me."

"Max, you're seriously going to make me cry," Mia said, sniffling. "Give me your damn bandanna, will you?" Mia blew her nose in it, and they both laughed.

"All right already. Are you going to open the damn box or what?"

"Yes… okay, I'm opening it." Mia gingerly pulled off the bow and unwrapped a white rectangular box. Inside, she found two porcelain figurines. One was a delicately winged blond nymph. She held the world in the palm of her hands. It was stunning. The other was a beautiful blond woman with a camera around her neck, on crutches, with the word GRACE written at the base. Mia burst out laughing at the sight of it. "Are you trying to tell me something, smart-ass? And where in the world did you find these?"

Max laughed. "They're custom made, but I am trying to make a point. In all sincerity, the first statue is what I really think of you. You're exquisite and delicate. You have everything going for you. The world is your oyster, so run with it. You deserve the best life has to offer, Mia. The second statue is just a reminder to keep your ego in check. Don't forget how I rescued that clumsy photographer rolling down the hill with dirt and twigs in her mouth and hair. She was also swearing like a sailor while she tumbled, hitting every log and rock. I thought GRACE was an appropriate name after all."

Mia chuckled as she brushed away the tears of happiness. "I love you, Max, even though you're absolutely crazy. Don't forget, we're friends forever." She hugged him and kissed his cheek.

"I love you too, Mia. You've given me hope for the future."

***

Vic saw the last few seconds between Max and Mia. She witnessed the hugs and kisses. She heard the expressions of love as she stood hidden from sight, behind the side gate. Tears pooled in her eyes then dropped to wet her tank top. She turned and walked back to the party on the patio—the party that was meant for Mia and Aaron.

Chapter Seventeen

Darkness filled the evening sky as the festivities were winding down. The music volume was set lower, and the drinking and merriment mellowed. The outdoor hanging lights illuminated the backyard, creating enormous shadowy figures from the giant oaks. Friends lingered because nobody wanted to call it a night. The group relaxed around the fire pit, each with a beverage in hand. Couples sat side by side, fingers intertwined, yet Vic found a reason to sit next to Tina instead of Max.

Sasha described the house she planned to buy in Aaron's neighborhood. The crowd oohed and aahed at the image she painted of it. She'd find out by Monday what the owners thought of her offer, according to Josh Redmond. Everyone laughed at the mention of his name. The ribbing and Redmond jokes lasted for fifteen minutes.

"He isn't *that* bad anymore. He just needed to be put in his place a little, and I took care of it," Sasha said proudly. "After knocking his ego down a few notches, he began working in a very professional manner," she added in Josh's defense.

"Uh oh... he got to her with his slimy charm," one neighbor replied, laughing.

"No, he didn't. I don't have any feelings toward Josh Redmond. This is a professional relationship and nothing more," Sasha said.

"Yeah, you watch," Morey said. "Soon enough, he's going to ask you out, especially if the house deal goes through. You'll owe it to him, in his mind. That's the way Josh rolls, honey. He does it to every woman he meets."

"Eww... you're grossing me out right now, Morey. I don't want to talk about Josh. All I'm saying is that the house could be mine very soon. It's about the house, nothing else."

"Yeah right, we'll see."

Mario elbowed Vic. He lifted his eyebrows and tipped his head toward Max as if to ask what was up between them. Vic shrugged her shoulders and brushed it off. She'd talk to her brother about it later.

***

Max tried to get Vic's attention, but she avoided eye contact with him. *What the hell is going on? Why is she ignoring me?*

He was confused by her lack of interest over the last few hours. He didn't want to say anything in front of the guests, so when she excused herself to make a pot of coffee, Max followed her inside. She busied herself in the kitchen, her back turned to him. Max sat at the table and waited for her to sit down, but Vic wouldn't stop moving. She poured the water in the pot, her hands shaking from nerves. She loaded the coffee filter with grounds and hit the ON button. She reached into the upper cabinet and pulled out every coffee cup.

"Vic? What's wrong? Are you mad at me for something? Can we talk?"

"The guests are waiting outside, Max. We can't sit in the kitchen and ignore them. There's nothing wrong—I'm fine."

"I'm not fine. You're pulling away from me tonight for some reason. Whatever this is needs to be discussed, and the sooner the better. If there's some misunderstanding between us, I want to fix it." Max rose from the table and walked over to her. He placed his hands gently on her shoulders. Her eyes were laser fixed on the coffeemaker. She wouldn't turn around. Max continued talking as he set a large tray on the counter top and placed the coffee cups, spoons, sugar, and creamer on it. "Please talk to me. I don't want to end the night this way, not knowing what's wrong."

"I've already said nothing's wrong." Vic opened the second drawer on the right and pulled out a hot pad. The coffeepot beeped, signaling it was full. Vic lifted the carafe by the handle and stabilized it from beneath with the hot pad. "Are you coming?" she asked as she walked toward the patio doors without looking back.

Max followed her only because he had the tray with the cups and condiments in his hands. He decided on one cup of coffee for the road, then he'd leave. It didn't seem like he would get any answers from Vic tonight, and waiting for everyone to go home wasn't an option because Max had no idea how late that would be. The ride home wasn't long, just a half hour, but he had his motorcycle, and the roads were dark. He drank the coffee, had a piece of cake with the remaining stragglers, and said good night.

***

The two-lane state highway was devoid of traffic. Other than Max's solitary headlight guiding him to Peekskill, pitch darkness filled the winding road. The deep rumble of his Harley was the only sound on that lonely stretch of highway. He was thankful for that cup of coffee, realizing it was two in the morning and he'd needed something to counteract the quantity of beer he drunk. Thoughts of Vic distracted him as he drove. *I want a relationship and a family. I'm thirty-seven years old, for God's sake. I think I'm a decent guy, but she's pushing me away for some reason.* His mind overflowed with doubt. *Maybe I should forget about her and go back to enjoying what I've been doing for thirteen years. The kids love me, and I have a great time with them on the hiking trails. I was content until I met Mia and Vic. I hadn't even thought about a relationship until then.*

He leaned into the curve of the road, but saw, too late, a shape ahead of him. He hit the brakes. A deer stood frozen in the middle of the road. There wasn't enough time to swerve as he skidded into it, hitting it dead center. Max flew over the handlebars and landed in a brush-filled ditch. He lay buried among the weeds, motionless, and time moved too slowly.

***

He gave a low-pitched groan as he regained consciousness. He opened his eyes to total darkness. Max reached into his pocket to retrieve his cell phone then realized he'd put it in the saddlebag of his motorcycle before driving away. *Shit! I need my phone, but it's so dark I'll never find it.* Max knew he wasn't okay. His legs and head were throbbing. He reached up and felt a wet, sticky substance matting his hair. Blood soaked his scalp and pooled in his ears. Max was sure he had a significant head injury. *There has to be a way to get to my bike before I pass out.* Sharp, agonizing pains shooting through his legs made it impossible to stand. The throbbing in his head and buzzing in his ears intensified until he lost consciousness again.

***

They cautiously drove the dark road after a night out with friends. Billy and Erica Mathis had ten miles to go before they reached home and the comfort of their king-sized bed. They were tired. Billy drove with his brights on since this stretch of road between towns was remote and dark.

"What the hell is that?" He tapped the brakes when he rounded the curve. He slowed down to see a deer lying dead in the middle of the road.

"That could really be dangerous, Billy. Anyone could hit it."

"Well, evidently somebody did." Billy stopped the car in the road with the headlights shining directly at the deer.

"Look, Erica, there's a skid mark and debris here. We have to take a closer look. I need to get the car off the road first." He backed the car up until he reached the gravel shoulder. Billy jumped out and left the headlights on, aiming directly at the deer. "Grab the flashlight out of the glove box, babe. Let's check this out." He realized as they got closer that the skid mark came from a single row of tires. "This had to be a motorcycle accident. Hitting a deer on a bike can't have a good outcome. We'd better look around."

They called out but only heard a lone owl hooting in the night. It was eerily quiet along that dark road. Billy scanned the shoulder and noticed ruts caused by something going off into the woods. He aimed the flashlight in that direction and saw the gleam of chrome bouncing off his light. "Over here. I think I found the motorcycle. Call 911—this can't be good." They ran through the brush toward the motorcycle as Erica dialed.

"Hello, my name is Erica Mathis, and my husband and I just came upon an accident on State Highway 9.... we're halfway between Sleepy Hollow and Peekskill. I have no idea how many people are involved. A motorcycle hit a deer, but we haven't found the driver yet. Please, you have to send an ambulance. We already found the motorcycle, but nobody was near it."

She finished the call and hung up. "Billy, he says we need to stay put and not touch anything. And we're supposed to keep calling out and listening for a response. They'll be here in fifteen minutes. Should we drag the deer off the road so nobody hits it again?"

"The dispatcher said not to touch anything, hon, we'll just shine the headlights if we see anyone approaching. That's all we can do for now."

Two squad cars arrived within ten minutes. Billy flagged them down while Erica kept searching near the Harley. The officers pulled off to the side of the road, set up flares, and got as much information as possible from the couple. They'd brought handheld spotlights, and the search began. Within minutes, the sound of sirens got closer. All told, there were seven people searching for the bike rider. With no luck in the vicinity of the bike, they widened the search area. Ten minutes later, one of the officers heard a muffled sound coming from behind them.

"Everyone, stop what you're doing and listen," he said anxiously.

They stopped moving and listened, ears perked. They were afraid to take a breath or snap a twig. Again, a groan sounded behind them.

"Back here," the officer said, aiming the spotlight toward the ditch behind them.

They carefully walked the shoulder, pointing their lights in the ditch, until they saw him.

"Here he is. Get the paramedics over here, and hurry!"

One of the paramedics backed the ambulance closer to where Max lay. They rushed over to check his condition as the deputies held the lights for them.

"Okay, he's in rough shape. We need the gurney over here. He has multiple deep lacerations on his head and face. Let's get a collar around his neck and slide the backboard under him. Let's go, guys!"

They determined by the man's mumbling that he was riding alone. When they finally got him in the light of the ambulance, they assessed his injuries. He had a concussion and needed a lot of stitches to stop the bleeding. There were numerous cuts and abrasions on his face and scalp. Both of his legs were broken. His torn jeans exposed the snapped tibia bone on his right leg and broken femur on the left. Several ribs were cracked, too. In the ambulance, he mumbled the name Vic.

***

The man was rushed to Hudson Valley Hospital Center where he was admitted, his broken bones were set, and he was placed in ICU. The doctors feared he might have bruised his brain. His head injuries were serious, and he hadn't been wearing a helmet. Fortunately, he didn't suffer any spinal injuries, but he needed to remain sedated until the swelling in his head went down. Without his cell phone, the police had no idea who to call.

Chapter Eighteen

Vic was still angry and hurt when she got up Sunday morning. *Damn them! The party could have been perfect. I wanted it to be perfect for Mia and Aaron—I really did. Why did Max and Mia have to go off together? Why did they say they loved each other?*

She stood by the patio doors and stared blankly at the backyard, the remnants of the party still lying around. The events of the night before played out in her mind, over and over, like a movie she couldn't turn off. *What am I doing wrong? I was sure Max wanted me until I saw Mia and him together in the driveway.* Vic held the steaming cup of coffee between her hands and wondered if she should confront them or not. *Why would Mia do this to Aaron? She told me there was nothing between her and Max. Would Mia lie to me, her best friend?* Vic made up her mind. She had to talk to Mia. She wasn't going to let this problem fester and turn into something bigger. *Better to confront it head-on and see what happens.*

A knock on the door sounded just as Vic passed the foyer on her way to the bedroom. She was going to get dressed and head directly to Mia's house. She tightened the belt on her bathrobe, made sure the chain lock was fastened, and opened the door slightly. Mia stood there.

"What the hell, Mia? It's eight thirty in the morning," she said, almost annoyed.

"Hey, girl, I came to help you clean up after last night. To be honest, I wanted to know what was going on with you and Max, too."

"What does that mean?" Vic asked, irritated by Mia's nosy, yet innocent, attitude.

"It smells like you made coffee. Can we sit and talk? Something was up with you guys last night. You weren't yourself. You were aloof and almost to the point of ignoring him. What gives? This isn't like you. Talk to me, sister." Mia helped herself to a cup of coffee. She pulled the bottle of creamer out of the refrigerator and placed it on the table next to her cup. She seemed to be preparing for a whole coffeepot's worth of conversation.

***

"I was aloof?" Vic said. "That's funny. What do you expect from me? You were my best friend, damn it."

"What the hell are you talking about? I *am* your best friend. Always was and always will be…"

"Do I really need to spell it out for you, Mia?"

"Well… yeah, I guess I do, because I'm at a disadvantage here. You're going to make me cry in a minute if you don't say what's on your mind. Now go ahead, just say it." Mia was getting nervous. Her right eye began twitching. *Damn tics. Why the hell is Vic pissed at me?*

"Fine… I'll blurt it out if that's what you want."

"That's what I want." Mia gulped her coffee, hoping it would settle her nerves. Vic was a Puerto Rican fireball after all. *I wonder if she's going to beat the shit out of me.*

"Okay, I'm talking about you and Max. I heard you guys saying how much you loved each other last night. There, I said it. Damn you, Mia. Why can't I have him for myself?"

Mia spit a mouthful of coffee across the table and began choking. "What the friggin' hell are you talking about? Apparently, you had too much to drink last night because my memory is of a nice evening spent with Aaron. Have you gone insane?"

"You two were in the driveway, hugging each other. You said you loved him, and he said it back. How do you explain that any other way than the way it was? Knock yourself out. Go ahead—tell me." Vic opened the cabinet and took out a wineglass. She pulled the stopper from a nearly empty bottle of Merlot that was left over from the party. She was disgusted at how little wine remained in the bottle. "Screw it," she said angrily and guzzled the contents right from the bottle.

"Really, Vic, it isn't even nine o'clock."

"You're not only a boyfriend stealer, now you're the wine police?" Vic snarled.

"Sit the hell down, and listen to me. I don't want any drama or interruptions, either. Jeez, Vic, get a grip. You're going to feel really stupid after I explain everything."

"I doubt it."

"Shush. Max asked me to come out to the driveway because he had a gift for me."

"Wow, that's awesome, Mia. What am I, friggin' chopped liver?"

"Vic... please, the gift was only out of friendship—nothing more. Max gave it to me as a thank-you for introducing you to him. He was happy and excited about his potential future with you. Yes, we did express our love... as friends. It's no different than you loving Aaron. I've told you before: Max is going to be in my life as a friend. I want all of us to be friends with each other—you know, our group?"

"Did he really say that—about me, I mean?" Tears welled up in Vic's eyes as she got up and opened a new bottle of wine. She poured two glasses and handed one to Mia. She sat down and cupped her head in her hands. "Oh my God, I can't believe what a jealous idiot I am. Can you ever forgive me?"

"People often believe what they see without knowing the facts. I did the very same thing to Aaron a few months ago. Luckily, we loved each other enough to talk through my insecurities. It turned out what I thought I saw was opposite from the truth. I felt like a fool because I didn't trust him enough at the time. I didn't have the facts, but now I know better. If anything ever appears off to you, you need to confront it immediately. Don't wait around and let it eat at you."

"I'm such a horse's ass. I probably screwed things up with Max forever. I ignored him last night, and he had no idea why."

"Call him, and be honest. He really cares about you. Do it now while you still have the courage. I'll start cleaning up the backyard." Mia walked outside and closed the patio door behind her. Vic needed privacy. Mia looked back through the slider and smiled, giving her a thumbs-up.

***

Shit. I'm so nervous. What the hell am I going to say? How do I begin? Vic searched for the right words as Max's phone rang. *I'll just start talking like I always do.*

The phone rang again. On the third ring it picked up, and Vic heard his sexy voice. "Hi, Max here."

"Hi, Max, it's Vic. I hope you enjoyed the party and…" Vic paused, realizing it was his recorded message talking, not Max in the flesh. *Damn it! It isn't really him.* She started over. "Hi, Max, it's Vic. I wanted to talk a bit. Hope your Sunday morning is going well. Give me a call… okay, bye." *Ugh… that sounded like shit.*

Vic joined Mia in the backyard with two fresh cups of coffee. Drinking wine at this time of day was just stupid and impulsive. "Let's sit and have some good, strong coffee. Sorry about the wine—that was dumb. Anyway, I got Max's voicemail, but I did leave a short message and asked him to call me back. I want to clear the air with him so we can move forward."

"That's good. Don't worry—everything will be okay. So, do you want to hang out after we clean up this mess? Aaron is teaching a photo-developing class today. Hey, where's Mario?"

"He's still asleep. It's kind of exciting that he and Max might open some stores together. They're so similar in that outdoorsy, hunky guy way. Even if Max is pissed off at me, I know he wants to get together with Mario. Somehow, we'll be able to fix things. I'm sure of it."

"All right, let's get this mess cleaned up and go bang on Tina and Sasha's door. Maybe they'll want to do lunch later."

"Sounds good, I love you, sister, and I'm sorry about everything."

Mia hugged her. "Vic, whenever you get insecure, just look in the mirror. You're the hottest, toughest babe in Westchester County."

Chapter Nineteen

Max lay in ICU under the watchful eyes of the hospital staff. He was in an induced coma due to the brain swelling. The bones in his legs were set, and his cuts were stitched. The only thing left to do was wait. The doctors identified Max from his driver's license, but they had no idea who to call. There wasn't a cell phone on him when he was brought to the hospital. Nobody was looking for him.

***

Orange cones narrowed the road to one lane as the tow-truck driver backed to the edge of the shoulder near the ravine. He wrapped a cable around Max's bike just beneath the handlebars. The winch was engaged, dragging the Harley through the brush and onto the flatbed truck owned by a garage in Peekskill. The bike was destroyed, reduced to a pile of rubble, ready for the junkyard.

The tow-truck driver didn't see the cell phone that had flown out of the saddlebag as the bike tumbled the night before. It lay in the weeds, hidden from sight. That cell phone contained the phone numbers of the people who cared about Max and his whereabouts. Max's only lifeline to those people lay forgotten along State Highway 9.

***

The girls gathered Monday morning at Hair Brained. Sasha and Karen sat on vacant styling chairs as Sasha waited anxiously for that important call from Josh Redmond. Today, she would find out if the owners of the Victorian on Sunrise Avenue had accepted or countered her offer. Mia had a photo shoot to do but agreed to join them for lunch at Morey's. Sasha paged through style magazine after style magazine, glancing at her watch regularly. She fidgeted and drank too much coffee.

"Sasha, you're going to go nuts if you don't settle down," Karen said. "Go ahead and call Josh to see if he found out anything."

"Won't that make me look desperate?"

"You already look desperate, for Pete's sake. He is supposed to be working for you, the buyer, remember? Just call him."

"Okay, I will in ten minutes. It's already eleven fifteen. He should know something by now. Look, I've bitten off my beautiful fingernails that Tina manicured so nicely, damn it!" Sasha asked Karen to check her hair for split ends. "*Pleeease*. I've got to get my mind off the house for a few more minutes."

"Oh, for crap's sake, Sasha." Tina grabbed the cell phone from Sasha's death grip and called Josh's office. As soon as it rang, she handed the phone back to Sasha. "Now, talk."

Sasha put on her assertive voice when he answered. "Josh, weren't you going to call me? What's up with the house?" The last thing Sasha wanted to do was give him the upper hand.

"Hey, Sasha, I was about to dial your number."

"Sure you were. So, what's their answer?"

"The owners laughed at the offer. I told you they would. I was embarrassed to even present it, but you insisted."

"Hey, Josh, your smart-ass attitude is showing through. Don't forget who you work for. If you don't sell that house, you don't get a commission, remember?" Sasha looked at the girls for approval. They giggled and gave her the thumbs-up. "Here's what I suggest you do," she continued. "Tell the owners to go to hell. Can you muster up the balls to do that for me?"

"What? You can't be serious."

"I'm as serious as a heart attack. They can go to hell, and you can join them. Good-bye, and thanks for nothing, Mr. Grossmond." Sasha punched the red End Call button with heavy emphasis. "Damn it. I wish I had a landline so I could slam the phone down on the receiver."

"What the hell? Did you really just say that, Sasha? You've got bigger balls than Vic does," Karen said, laughing. "And you called him Mr. Grossmond instead of Redmond. I love it, but what about the house? You want that place more than anything."

"Oh, I'll get that house. They're messing with the wrong person. And Josh can kiss my lovely ass. I'll find another realtor that takes me seriously." Sasha huffed. "I bet you guys anything Josh will come around like a puppy with his tail tucked between his legs. Mark my words—he'll be calling me back sometime today," she added proudly.

Lunch at Morey's was one of the girls' favorite activities. Not only was Morey a good friend, but the food at his pub rocked. They waited for Mia to show up on the newly added outdoor deck. The deck was constructed to the side and back of the building, giving patrons a chance to people watch as the tourists passed by or enjoy being near the beautiful, dense wooded area behind the restaurant. Bird feeders were randomly scattered in the back along with garden beds. The girls sat toward the front with the street view because they were watching for Mia. They ordered a pitcher of beer and talked a mile a minute.

"So, Vic, what's on the agenda for you and Max next weekend?" Karen asked as she leaned in, rubbing her hands together and giving Vic a wicked smile.

"Well, Ms. Nosy, I haven't spoken to Max since the party. I'm going to let him pursue me. You know, that's how you get guys to really want you. You have to come across as indifferent. I read *The Rules*," Vic said.

"Is that really true?" Sasha asked.

"Of course it is. The bitches always get the guys. It's so stupid."

"What is?" Sasha asked, as innocent as a teenage girl trying to land the pimply boy next door.

"It's like this. Guys *love* to bitch about how high maintenance their girlfriends or wives are, *but* those are the women they choose. For whatever reason, they need that drama and constant conflict in their lives. I guess it makes them feel more manly or something. It's so friggin' dumb."

"So, the only way to get a guy is by being a bitch to him?" Sasha asked.

"Yep," Karen, Tina, and Vic said.

"That means Josh Redmond is going to be all over me," Sasha said, giggling.

"Gross. Here comes our chicky mama. Hey, Mia, over here."

Sasha's phone began chirping as the five of them finished their lunch and beer. "Oh my God, it's Josh. He didn't waste any time." Sasha's felt excitement come over her as she answered her phone and listened to what he had to say. "Yes, uh-huh, okay… I'll get back to you in a few days. Good-bye, Mr. Redmond."

"Wow, you really are a hard-ass, Sasha. What did he want?" Mia asked, grinning. "Hang on. Lisa, can you bring us the check, please? Okay… what did Mr. Dickmond—oh sorry, I mean Mr. Redmond—say?"

"I knew it. All I had to do was play hardball with him. Now the owners have reconsidered my offer. I guess I scared them when I acted like I wasn't interested anymore. Anyway, Josh said they countered with $725,000. I'm going to let all of them sweat for two days. I'll present my final offer at $715,000 and not a penny more. I'll make sure Josh understands that, too."

"How did you get so real estate savvy?" Vic asked.

Sasha grabbed Karen and gave her a big hug. "Karen, dear friends, has become my personal real estate guru. She's been giving me excellent house-hunting advice ever since I moved to Tarrytown."

Tina shook her head in amazement, "No shit? You're a quick study, Sasha—I'll give you that."

***

The girls walked the five minutes back to Hair Brained. Mia eased Vic back by her arm to slow down their pace. She wanted to have a private conversation even though it would be short.

"Hey, what's going on with Max? Has he called you back?" Mia asked, lowering her voice as they walked.

"No, he hasn't. Damn it. It was too good to be true. Why do I always screw things up?"

"Well, first off, you don't. But the weird thing is that doesn't sound like him. He's too nice to behave that way. Something isn't sitting right with me. Has Mario tried calling him about the business stuff?"

"Yes," Vic said, "but Max hasn't returned his calls, either. Could he be that pissed at me to give up on a good business opportunity?"

"I'm not sure, hon. Are you going to try again? Do you want me to call him to see if he's screening his calls?"

"Max isn't stupid, Mia. He'll see right through that. I'll try again on Wednesday. Have you been to his house in Peekskill?"

"Nope, never. Sorry—I'm not much help. Let's talk later," Mia said as they entered the salon.

Mia left at two since she had one more photo shoot to do that afternoon. This one was at the town square for a child's third birthday. There would be moms, kids and a clown. Mia planned to take plenty of candid shots. *This should be a blast,* she thought as she stopped at her house to gather the photography equipment. The town square was full of colorful balloons hanging from the gazebo. Even the playground was decorated. Streamers draped from every available post. Adorable children ran around, squealing, as they chased each other in their designated area with helicopter moms hovering overhead. Mia laughed at the commotion as she carried her cameras to a picnic table covered in a cartoon-character tablecloth. There were enough hotdogs, chips, fruit, and juice lined up on the tables to feed a small nation. Mia spent two hours photographing children playing, eating, and crying. By the time she was done, they were all exhausted.

"Well, that was a riot." She said good-bye to the moms and drove home. *A hot bath sounds perfect right now.* Mia unloaded her car and went inside. *I'll walk Reggie first then relax in the tub.* "C'mon, Reg, let's go outside."

Reggie knew the routine. He loved the twice-a-day walks he and Mia shared. He waited anxiously by the front door, wagging his tail and whining, as Mia put the leash on his collar and jammed a baggie in her pants pocket. They took off down the sidewalk for the usual half-hour neighborhood walk.

"There. You're good for the night," Mia said, panting, as she and Reggie ran the last few blocks home.

She filled Reggie's stainless-steel water dish in the corner by the garage door then headed to the bathroom and turned on the water in the oversized Jacuzzi. *This is going to feel awesome.* The jets were set on high as the water continued to fill the bathtub. She undressed, stepped in, and sat back, relaxing while the powerful jets kneaded her achy muscles.

Mia heard a key turning the lock on the front door. The hinge squeaked as the door opened and closed. *I've got to spray some WD-40 on that hinge.* Reggie barked anxiously, and Mia heard Aaron's voice as he laughed and played with him in the foyer. She smiled. She loved those two so much and was grateful Aaron cared about Reggie as much as she did. Her mind flashed back to Jack and how indifferent he'd been with her precious dog. Mia had never trusted Jack to walk or care for Reggie in the three years she'd known him.

"Mia, honey, it's me. Where are you?"

"I'm enjoying a hot bath. I swear I've been thinking about this all day."

"What? You've been thinking about a bath and not me?" he joked.

"I've been thinking about this bath and you in it with me," she teased back.

"I like the sound of that." Aaron appeared at the bathroom door. He leaned against the frame and smiled.

"What?"

"Nothing. I just need to take in your beauty before I ravish you—that's all. I never thought my life could feel this complete until you came to your senses and divorced Jack." Aaron ducked as Mia threw the washcloth at him.

"Smart-ass," she said. "Get in here and wash my back."

"With pleasure, Ms. James."

Mia watched Aaron strip off his clothes. They lay in a pile on the floor, next to hers. "Just watching you undress gets me going. I'm the luckiest and horniest woman in Tarrytown right now."

"I thought you wanted me to wash your back. Isn't this a therapeutic bath?" He stepped in and knelt down in front of her.

"Oh, it's definitely therapeutic. You're going to knead and rub every inch of my aching body," Mia replied as she licked his neck slowly all the way up to his lips. She kissed him and pulled on his earlobe with her teeth. Aaron moaned when she found his growing shaft beneath the water and began caressing it.

"God, you drive me crazy."

"That's my goal in life, Aaron. I want to drive you crazy. You're going to lust after me forever."

"I've been lusting after you for twenty years already." He fondled her. Mia moaned when he reached that perfect spot between her legs.

"I want you so much, Aaron." She pulled him in closer,

positioning him between her legs. "Just take me, damn it. I can't hold on any longer. Fill me up, babe."

Aaron thrust his manhood into Mia and rocked her back and forth as the pounding jets created even more sexual energy between them. They climaxed in a fury of passion and churning water.

***

Mia rested against Aaron's shoulder, her wet hair draped across his chest. They lay in bed, each sipping a glass of wine.

"Your divorce will be final before long, honey. Everyone in town knows we're together, especially since the party. How about moving in with me? You love my house probably even more than I do." Aaron stroked Mia's hair and kissed her forehead.

"Do you think it's appropriate given the timing? This is a small town, and we have our business reputations to think of."

"That's true, but it isn't like we just met. Everyone living in Tarrytown loves you, and they know Jack wasn't right for you. He was a Manhattan snob who didn't belong here to begin with. My business is strong and stable. Nobody would judge us, Mia. It's our life to do what makes us happy. I'm going to marry you as soon as your divorce is final if you'll have me. That makes us as legit as they come."

"Was that a proposal, Aaron Daniels?"

"Nope. When you get a proposal from me, you'll know

it, babe. There's going to be a citywide party with fireworks and live music."

Mia laughed. "You're crazy, Aaron."

"Yeah, crazy in love."

Chapter Twenty

"Damn it all!" Vic pouted.

"What's wrong?" Tina asked as she painted Sasha's nails. Sasha had chewed off her manicure a few days earlier from sheer nerves about the Victorian.

"I just forgot to do something." Vic walked out the front door, carrying her cell phone. "I'll be right back." She didn't want the girls overhearing the call she was making to Max. She hoped he would finally answer. Vic walked around to the back of the salon and sat at the small table in the shade, in a chair facing the salon so she'd know if anyone came out looking for her. She silently said a little prayer, hoping Max would answer. She pressed the green telephone icon next to his name and waited. The ringing was enough to set her nerves in motion. Vic's mouth went dry. *Damn it. Why didn't I bring a bottle of water outside with me?* The phone rang again. The third ring went to voicemail, his sexy voice giving a recorded greeting. It happened again. *Where the hell is he? There's no way he wouldn't answer after four days. Even if he's still mad at me, wouldn't he at least let me explain?* Vic began to feel uneasy about the whole situation. She and Mia didn't know Max that well. *Could he be that much of a jerk?* Vic pushed the chair back and got up to go inside, but decided to make a quick call to Mia instead. She tapped her long, hot-pink fingernails on the table.

"Chica, I tried Max's phone again, and there's still no answer. What the hell should I do?"

"Jeez, I'm at a loss here. It doesn't feel right, knowing how sweet Max usually is."

"I'm starting to freak out, Mia. It isn't about our so-called relationship, either. I'm worried that something is actually wrong."

"I'm with you, sister. Come over after work. We've got to figure this out."

"Thanks, hon. I can always count on you."

"I love you," Mia said. "I have your back, so take a deep breath. We'll get to the bottom of things—I promise. Later, ciao."

"Thanks." Vic was happier walking back into the salon. *Mia will figure this out.* Mrs. Abraham was reading a magazine at the shampoo bowl, waiting for Vic to wash her hair. "Hello, Mrs. Abraham. I hope I didn't keep you waiting too long. Let's get started, shall we?"

***

Mia checked the time. It was five o'clock. *Vic should be arriving any time now.* Too anxious to sit down, Mia chose to pace the kitchen floor. Reggie's head followed her movements as if he were watching a tennis match. Back, forth, back, forth. He began to whine, sensing Mia's anxiety. "Sorry, Reg, I'm probably making you dizzy." She tried to think of a logical reason why Max would avoid Vic at all costs, but she couldn't come up with anything. The screeching sound of rims scraping the curb in front of her house brought her to the kitchen window. She saw Vic's car jammed against the curb, the rims scraped for the millionth time. "Eww... that's not good," Mia said, cringing.

Vic got out of her car, walked around to the passenger side, and began swearing in Spanish. Mia burst out laughing. "Vic, you're nothing if not predictable," she yelled out the open window.

Vic stormed up the sidewalk and into the house, both hands throwing wild gestures in the air. "Son of a bitch. Why do I hit the friggin' curb every time I park?"

"Why don't you just pull into the driveway? There's plenty of room."

"How the hell do I know what I'm going to do? Anyway, hi. Let's have some wine and try to figure out what to do about Max. I swear I'll go as stark raving mad as a squawking loon if I don't get the chance to apologize to him and get things back on track."

"Huh?"

"Never mind." Vic grabbed two wineglasses out of Mia's liquor cabinet.

Mia had several bottles of Merlot on the table and Chardonnay in the fridge as a backup. They sat at the table, and Vic poured.

"Okay… how do we find out if Max is mad and not answering or if something is actually wrong? He won't pick up my calls or Mario's. It won't work if you call, and he isn't acquainted with the rest of the clan well enough to even answer the phone."

"Well, that's it, then. We can block the caller ID and have Karen try. He wouldn't recognize her voice, and she can ask for a nonexistent person. It would seem like an innocent wrong number."

"Yeah, that's all great, but then Karen would want to know why we're pulling this charade. I'm too embarrassed to tell her why Max isn't returning my calls."

"Shit… you're right. So, if our main objective is to make sure he's alive and well, we could stalk him like we did to Jack and Sasha. At least we'll see if he's okay. That would tell us he isn't answering his phone on purpose. I'd take it from there after that and act as a mediator."

"You'd do that for me?"

"Of course I would. The problem is, we don't have a clue where Max lives. The only thing I remember from talking to him casually is he lives in Peekskill. There are twenty-five thousand people in that town, and we have no idea if he lives in the city or the country. Somehow, there has to be a way to track down his address. He only has a cell phone, so we can't look him up in the phone book. We've never talked at length about his family, so I'm at a loss if he has any around here. Cole is a pretty common last name, too. Shit, we're screwed!"

"What if we call every Cole in the phone book?

Someone might be related to Max. Let's check it out. Where are your phone books?"

"I'm not sure if I have any. Grab a stool and open the cabinet above the refrigerator."

Vic found three phone books. She was excited until she saw the dates on them. "Really, Mia, for crap's sake—these are ancient. Where are the newer ones?"

"They don't deliver phone books anymore, do they? How old are those?"

"They're from 2002, 2006, and 2009. What happened to the years in between?"

"Who the hell knows? Reggie probably ate them. Bring 2009 over here, and let's check that one. But first, let's have another glass of wine and settle our nerves."

"Good plan, mama."

The room grew quiet as both girls retracted into their own thoughts. The only sound was the constant ticking of the wall clock above the antique kitchen set that Mia had inherited from her grandparents. They slugged down the wine in three gulps. "Pour some more, Mia. I'm afraid to look at the phone books. I don't want to be let down."

"I know—I'm nervous too."

With a little alcoholic confidence stirring them up, they paged through the Cs and found Cole listed four times in Peekskill.

"That's depressing. I thought there would be more. This isn't going to take long. Okay, here goes. Read me the first number."

Mia read the first phone number as Vic punched it

into her cell. It was disconnected. The second number was a recorded message from Alan and Betty Cole, and the voice—probably Betty's—sounded like it belonged to a ninety-year-old woman. Vic left a short message saying if they were related to Max Cole, to call her phone number. The third number went to someone whose last name wasn't Cole—apparently, that phone number had been given to someone else years ago. Vic made the last call, and a male voice picked up. It turned out to be a third cousin of Max's named Bobby Cole. He said he hadn't seen Max since they were in their early twenties because they ran in different crowds. Mia understood what that meant. He told her that back in the mid-90s, Max had lived in a small apartment above the hardware store downtown. The family homestead was sold in 1995. Bobby thought Max had left town and moved to Utah in 2004. Vic thanked him for his time and hung up. They'd struck out completely. The girls looked at each other in defeat.

"He's a ghost, Mia, a real enigma. Why don't we have a damn clue about someone we care for? What the hell is wrong with us?"

"There's nothing wrong with us," Mia said. "We've only known Max for a couple of months. It takes time to build relationships."

"I know, but…"

"But what?"

"But… I'm falling in love with him."

Mia took Vic's hand in hers. She saw the anguish in her best friend's face. This Puerto Rican babe, this tough broad, was breaking. Her vulnerabilities were coming out. The hard edge she was so proud of was melting away. Tears from both of them fell to the table.

Chapter Twenty-One

"We'll find him," Mia said. "Let's Google how many towns between here and Peekskill have police departments. We'll call them and ask if there were any serious accidents reported since Saturday after midnight."

"Will they tell us anything if we aren't family?"

"I'm not sure, but we have to try."

Down the hall, to the left of the master bedroom, was Mia's office. It was the same office Jack used to sneak away to late at night and send steamy emails to Sasha. That time seemed so long ago, yet Mia still flinched at the thought of it. *Now's not the time to think of that jerk.* She turned on the computer and sat in the large leather office chair. She pointed to the side chair at the far end of the room. "Grab that chair and sit down next to me." Vic obliged, and Mia began a Google search. She typed in a map search for the towns between Tarrytown and Peekskill. Vic waited with a pad of paper and pen in hand as she repositioned herself in the chair.

"Wait a minute," Mia said, leaning in closer to the computer monitor. "What's this?"

She pulled up the Incident & Congestion Report for the Hudson Valley area of New York, Connecticut, New Jersey, Pennsylvania, and Massachusetts. "There might be something here. I can click on New York and then the county. Let's see what comes up."

Mia was a bad typist, usually tapping away with her index fingers, but at the moment, that didn't matter. It would only take a few minutes to check the website. With two sets of eyes scanning the entries back to Saturday night, the search went a lot faster. Most of the posts were road-condition incidents such as potholes that needed repair or debris on the road. Halfway down the page, they both saw the accident report at the same time. Their backs stiffened in their chairs. They gasped together as they read about a motorcyclist hitting a deer on State Highway 9 just north of Croton-on-Hudson. The call had come in Sunday morning at about two thirty from a passing motorist.

"No!" Vic began sobbing uncontrollably. Her entire body shook in despair. "It's Max—it has to be. Who else would be on a motorcycle at that time, on that road? Oh my God, I can't believe this."

"Okay, Vic, we need to find out for sure if it was him. C'mon, let's go." By this time, Mia was well on her way to breaking down, too, but she knew somebody had to be strong and in control.

"Where are we going?" Vic cried out.

"Croton-on-Hudson's police department, we need information. Clean yourself up a little. I have to call Aaron and see if he'll come over and take care of Reggie until we get back. Now, hurry! Go run some cold water over your face. You'll feel better."

They were on their way within ten minutes. Mia drove as responsibly as she could. Once they got out of town she had to check herself often. Every time she looked at the speedometer she was going at least twenty miles per hour over the speed limit. "Damn it! Why don't I have cruise on this hunk of shit? I'm going to end up getting a ticket, I swear."

"Mia, don't call this car a hunk of shit. You love it."

"I'm just frustrated."

Dusk was setting in. Mia remembered from plenty of nature shots that deer often came out to eat in the early evening. Twilight was right around the corner. She had to be careful on these winding roads. Because of the tree cover, the stretch between Sleepy Hollow and Croton-on-Hudson was dark even in the middle of the day. The heavy, ancient oaks engulfed her car like a shroud as Mia drove. She slowed down because she had to. They would arrive at the police station in fifteen minutes as long as she remained cautious and kept her eyes peeled for anything on the road.

"We're getting close," she said. "Find the police station's address on your cell. Guide me in."

"Got it—I can do that." Vic pulled up Google maps and found the address. "It's 1 Van Wyck Street. We exit Highway 9 onto South Riverside Avenue. It's a frontage road. We stay on that until we come to Brook Street. We turn right and go all the way to Old Post Road. We'll make a right there too, and go one block. The Municipal Building is on the corner. It sounds easy enough."

"Okay, here's Riverside. We'll be there in a minute," Mia said as she turned onto Brook Street. "Here's the parking lot. Let's go. Are you going to be all right? I'm not sure if they'll tell us anything, so let's try to remain calm, and don't go all commando on them, okay?"

"Okay, Chica."

They held hands as they power walked to the entrance and found the police department down the hall on the right. They pushed through the double glass doors and approached the counter.

"Excuse me. Who do we speak to about accident reports?" Mia asked politely.

"Are you reporting an accident?" the desk officer asked.

"No, we're looking for someone who may have been involved in an accident Saturday night. We just want someone to confirm that it was, or wasn't, our friend."

"So, you aren't related to the person you're looking for?"

Son of a bitch, why did I say that? "Um… no, but she's engaged to him. His name is Max Cole." *White lies run out of my friggin' mouth like water. I'm really getting good at telling them. Sorry, Jesus. I'll go to church next Sunday—I promise.*

"Have a seat. Someone will be out in a few minutes to talk to you." The officer gave them both the once-over then disappeared around the corner.

"I can't sit down." Vic walked the length of the counter fifteen times before another officer came out and introduced himself.

"Ladies, I'm Officer Moreno. What can I do for you?"

Mia gave him a quick assessment. *He doesn't look like a complete jerk. He's not puffing out his chest with a full-of-himself attitude. He does have a pot gut, and that handlebar mustache—what the hell is that crusty stuff on it? Oh well... he'll have to do.* "We were wondering about an accident that was called in Saturday night, or actually Sunday morning to be specific. It was about a motorcyclist hitting a deer."

"Yes, I'm familiar with that accident. Are you family?"

"Well, no, but it is public information. The report was on the Internet."

"It didn't state the victim's name though, did it? If it had, you wouldn't be here asking."

"Victim?" Vic went into a round of hysterics at the sound of the word.

"Ma'am, you need to compose yourself. Victim is the generic term used for anyone involved in an accident. It does not mean he's deceased. Now, what relationship do you both have with this person?"

"I'm a close friend and..."

"I'm his fiancée. We're getting married in a few months. I'm pregnant with his baby!" Vic wailed.

Mia's head spun around so fast it almost shot off her shoulders. *Damn girl—you're good!*

"It's Wednesday night. You're just looking for him

now?" the officer asked, becoming suspicious.

"We had a fight, okay? I was giving him space, but it's been too long." Vic was sobbing so hard she was almost unable to speak. Mia hugged her and patted the top of her head.

"I'll take over, hon. Breathe like they taught you in Lamaze class. Officer, please help us. We only want to know if the person involved in that accident was Max Cole, and where he is right now. We'll leave as soon as we get that information. You don't want this sobbing, irrational, pregnant woman sitting here all night, do you?" *I might as well jump on the preggers bandwagon.*

He gave each of them an irritated look and asked for their driver's licenses. "I'll be back with these in a minute. If there are any disturbances in town from either of you, we'll be knocking on your doors." Officer Moreno walked into a small room where the copy machine was located. He took two more quick bites of his glazed donut. He returned with their licenses and sat down nearest Mia. *Something is telling me to stay out of reach of the pregnant Puerto Rican.* "Okay, ladies, I have confirmation that the person in the accident on State Highway 9 early Sunday morning was indeed Max Cole." He flinched in defense as Vic's arms began flailing wildly. "What in God's name?" He ducked for the second time. "Please control your friend, or I'll have to restrain her. As I was saying, the motorcyclist was Max Cole, and he was transported to Hudson Valley Hospital Center in Peekskill immediately after the accident. Would you like me to call and see if he's still a patient there?"

"Yes, please. That would be so helpful," Mia replied as politely as she could. "Vic," she whispered, "take it down a notch before he locks us up. We'll be out of here in five minutes. Just control yourself, for crap's sake."

"I can't help myself. I'm PMSing, Mia. You know, the mood swings and all?"

"That would be funny if this wasn't so serious."

"You're right, and I'm sorry. I won't make another peep."

The officer returned and informed the girls that Max was still listed as a patient. He didn't think they would be allowed to see him since he was in ICU. Visitation in ICU was normally reserved for family only. "Give it a shot, and good luck. Take your time getting there, too. You don't want to be detained with a speeding ticket tonight, right, ladies?"

"Yes, you're right, officer. Thank you very much for your help. Goodbye." Mia shook his hand. They turned and bolted out the door toward the parking lot.

Chapter Twenty-Two

"Vic, find the address of Hudson Valley Hospital Center in Peekskill just like you did for the police station earlier. We should be there in about ten minutes."

Vic was so nervous her hands shook as she tried to type the name of the facility into the Google search bar. "Son of a bitch," she screeched. "I can't even spell simple words that a second grader could right now."

"Use Google microphone, and just say what you're looking for. Make it easy on yourself, for Pete's sake. I've got to keep my eyes on the road."

"Shit, that's right. Sorry, Chica. Okay, hang on. I've got to breathe first. All right, stay on Highway 9 until you get to the South Street ramp. Turn right on South Street until you come to South Division Street. That turns into Crompond Road, which will take us right to the hospital driveway."

"Okay, just keep guiding me till we get there."

Mia parked in the emergency-room lot. They rushed into the hospital entrance and up to the counter. Vic was already wailing again. The startled looks on the faces of the ladies behind the reception counter put everyone on alert. They gave a heads-up glance in the direction of the security guards.

"Vic, calm the hell down. I'll do the talking, or we'll get kicked out of here before we find out anything." Mia put on her best smile and took a deep breath. She told Vic to sit in the waiting area and not move, or speak, until she came back for her and then approached the front desk. "Hello there. I'm hoping you can help us. My friend and I were told her fiancé is a patient here. His name is Max Cole. We're aware he's in ICU and there are strict rules as far as visitors go, but he has nobody else here. His fiancée, the crying woman over there, is pregnant with his child. Please, you have to help us." Mia noticed how easily she'd blurted out another lie. She smiled pitifully and waited. Calming elevator music played in the background. There were obvious shades of green on the walls, meant to relax visitors and patients. *I need to remind Vic of that.*

One of the ladies behind the counter rose, scowled, and said she would be right back. She soon returned with a security guard and said they could go up to see Max. "Any ruckus, incidents, or outbreaks of crazy, and both of you ladies will have to leave. The security guard will immediately extract you from the building. Is that clear?"

"Yes, ma'am, we'll behave—I promise."

Mia waved to get Vic's attention. Vic ran over to join her. The silence in the elevator was deafening as they were led up to the fourth floor. The music played quietly through the speakers. The guard gave them both the shit eye. "Follow me," he said as the elevator doors opened.

They were led down several hallways until they arrived at the ICU wing. A large counter with people hustling about was directly in front of them. "I'm going to wait up here for you. Don't make me throw you out, understand?"

"Yes, we understand," Mia replied, nodding. She grabbed Vic's hand and held her close. "Excuse me, we would like to see Max Cole." *Be assertive but polite.*

"And you are?" the nurse asked with her head cocked to the side.

"I'm a friend that drove his fiancée here. She's pregnant." *Damn it. This whole preggers thing is taking on a life of its own.*

"Please take a seat. His doctor will come out and talk to you."

The girls sat and waited. The soft background music echoed through the hospital hallways. They stared into space, not knowing what else to do. "Do you want some coffee?" Mia asked.

"Yeah, that sounds good, thanks." Vic quietly cried into her hands, not wanting to upset the guard or anyone else.

Within ten minutes, a typical-looking, middle-aged man in a white lab coat approached them. "I hear you're asking about Max Cole? One of you is his fiancée, is that correct?"

"Yes, I am," Vic replied, looking up with red, swollen eyes.

Mia couldn't believe the stories they were coming up

with. *Jeez... we're so going to hell for all the lies we've told in the last hour.*

"I'm Doctor Taylor. Mr. Cole has suffered considerable damage to both legs and has numerous stitches. Our main concern, though, is the swelling on his brain. That's why he's in ICU."

Tiny sobs and coughs came from Vic even though she was doing her best to suppress them. Tears streamed down Mia's cheeks.

"The good news is we've seen considerable progress over the last forty-eight hours. The swelling is going down. Right now, Mr. Cole is in an induced coma, but we're hoping to wake him up tomorrow. We'll do an MRI of his brain and see how things look then. What he needs is rest. His legs will heal of course, but they were both broken in multiple areas. He's wearing casts, and he'll be in a wheelchair for a while. Our focus and concern right now is his brain and if there is any permanent damage. There's really nothing else I can tell you."

"Can we see him?" Vic asked. "I just want to sit with him, please."

"Of course, but you have to remain calm. We don't know if subconsciously he hears you, but we don't want any loud noises that might startle him."

"Okay. Thank you, doctor. We'll be as quiet as possible."

Vic and Mia tiptoed into Max's room. The sight of him shook them both to the core. His face was deeply bruised and swollen. Stitches covered much of his body that was visible.

Both legs wore white casts. Max had every kind of monitor and alarm hooked up to him. IVs and tubes dangled from both arms. He lay asleep with no idea they were sitting next to him. Vic and Mia looked him over closely and whispered their anguish to each other. Vic gently touched his hand. It flinched lightly. The girls each said a silent prayer over him and walked out to the nurse's station.

"Will someone take down my name as a contact?" Vic asked. "I'd like to come back every evening, especially once he wakes up."

The nurses wrote down Vic and Mia's phone numbers and listed them as people allowed to visit.

The ride back to Tarrytown held disbelief and sadness for both women. Mia watched the dark road closely as she drove. Vic stared out the window into the blackness. "Mia?"

"Yeah?"

"Do you think Max had the accident because of me? Was he upset about the way I acted toward him Saturday night and not paying attention to the road?"

"Honey, don't put that burden on yourself. You'll never know what Max was thinking unless he tells you. It's not like he carelessly veered off the road. He hit a deer, and that's a big animal to be standing in the road. There wasn't enough time to react—that's all." Mia reached over and patted Vic's shoulder.

"I've learned a hard lesson."

"What's that?" Mia asked.

"Not to believe everything I see. There could be a totally innocent explanation for a lot of things people misinterpret. I should have spoken up. If I'd walked over to you guys on the driveway, I would have realized neither of you were doing anything wrong. I'll never, and I mean never, prejudge people again. I'm so sorry, Mia."

"It's okay. Now, all we have to do is pray for Max. Why don't you make a few phone calls while I drive? We need to tell everyone what's going on."

Back in the comfort of Mia's house, the two women slumped down on the couch, letting out spontaneous sighs. Aaron handed each of them a glass of chilled Chardonnay and sat next to Mia, comforting them both as they took turns explaining what they'd learned in the last few hours.

"I don't really know Max, but I'm so sorry he's going through this. If there's anything I can do to help, just say the word. Mia and I are there for you, Vic. The same goes for all our friends."

"Thanks. That means a lot. I'll probably be going to the hospital after work each night. I'd like it if everyone took turns going along. I think leaning on each other as he recovers will lessen the stress."

"I agree, hon. I'll do my photography around your work schedule. We'll go with you whenever you want. Max might recover quicker if he has stimulation from people he knows."

"Okay, guys, I'm beat. I need to go home. Stop in at lunchtime tomorrow, Mia. You can decide where to eat. Aaron, join us, please. It would be nice."

"Will do. Good night."

Chapter Twenty-Three

The next week went by slowly. Ninety percent of Vic's mind was on Max and ten percent on her job. Anything that could be critical, like hair coloring and cuts, was left in the capable and safer hands of Tina. Vic settled for taking care of the mani-pedis and rolling the little old ladies' hair in curlers. She didn't get much sleep and found her head bobbing plenty of times throughout the day.

Max was taken out of his induced coma five days later. He slept a lot on his own just because of the pain medication and didn't seem to recognize anyone who stopped in, especially Vic. She was the constant in that hospital room every night, but he still couldn't get a grasp on names or faces. Max worked with a speech and occupational therapist several times a day. His motor skills were improving, but he had a long, hard road ahead of him. Vic was diligent and loyal. She felt a true sense of love toward Max. She also felt an equal sense of guilt that she couldn't shake off.

***

The chimes on the grandfather's clock in the living room sounded three times. Vic tossed and turned in bed, irritated by her inability to sleep. Her eyes burned like hot pokers. She needed sleep, but she wouldn't get any without help. She stumbled out of bed and zombie walked to the kitchen. Sleepytime tea always made her dozy. With her eyes only open enough to see through the slits, she poured water into a cup, placed it in the microwave, and set the timer for two minutes then sat with her tea on the recliner and thought about Max. The TV was turned on as background noise with a middle-of-the-night "firm up your butt" infomercial playing. Vic stared at it but didn't see a thing. Her fingers grasped the tea bag string and mindlessly bobbed it up and down in the cup. *Will he ever remember me? Is his mind going to come back and function fully in time? I want to start over with him and show him I can be a sweet person. I don't have to be the hard-ass, insecure bitch. It isn't at all funny, or attractive, now that I think about it. Why don't I ever let the real me show? Why am I always hiding behind the tough-girl facade?*

Vic thought back to her childhood. It was hard being the only girl in a family of four kids. They definitely weren't privileged either. The family worked hard for everything they had. "The tough ones win, Vic," her dad always said. *Is that where it came from?* Vic took one last sip of tea as she watched the butt-firming exercises on TV. *This is such crap. I've got a firm butt anyway. It's time for bed.* She clicked off the remote and vowed to get some sleep.

Tuesday, Mario offered to go with Vic to the hospital. Everyone else had prior commitments or had to work during the day. Mario also volunteered to stay another week just to make life a little easier on Vic. She appreciated her baby brother so much. Vic was optimistic. The doctor told her Max would be moved to the neighboring rehabilitation center in two days. His condition was good, but he needed extensive mental and physical therapy while his brain and broken legs healed. They entered the room as Max was being helped with his lunch. His weak grasp caused him to drop the fork. The therapist handed it back to him. He dropped it again.

"I can do that," Vic volunteered happily. She sat on the edge of the bed and handed Max the fork each and every time he dropped it. Max stared at her then looked at Mario.

"How's it going, Mario?" he asked with a thick slur.

Vic dropped the fork. "Max, you recognized Mario. You remembered his name," she said excitedly.

He looked at her again, and with the heavy slur said, "Vic, you're here."

She sobbed openly as she pushed the food tray to the side and carefully hugged him. "I'm here, Max. I'll always be here for you. You can depend on me—I promise you that. Mario, get the doctor. They have to see his memory is coming around. This is such good news!"

They were asked to leave the room while the doctor checked Max over.

"Mario, text me as soon as the doctor comes out. I'm

going outside to call the girls. They'll be so excited to hear the news."

The doctor and therapists worked with Max for nearly an hour before they came out of the room. Mario and Vic waited on the edge of their seats.

"Max's brain function needs to be tested," the doctor said. "I would suggest going home and coming back in the morning. We'll be running him through quite a few tests throughout the day. Tomorrow, we'll have more information after we read the results. Go home and relax. It looks like today is going to be a long day, but I think the prognosis will please you."

"Thank you, doctor. We'll be back in the morning." Vic was on cloud nine as she and her brother drove home.

Everyone gathered for dinner at Vic's house. The girls brought all the food so Vic could sit back and enjoy the evening with her dearest friends. They toasted Max's imminent recovery.

"I don't want to make this night anything to do with me. We're celebrating Max, but I'm so happy I can't contain it anymore," Sasha said out of pure excitement. "I'll pee my pants if I don't just tell you."

"Hell no—we're not going to mop up your mess," Mia joked. "Just spill already."

"Okay… ready? The owners accepted my offer on the Victorian. Yay! Josh actually came through for me."

"Oh my God, Sasha, that's wonderful news. And Josh, um… the jury is still out on him, but tonight is a great night to celebrate. Does anyone else have something exciting to say?" Karen asked, grinning at everyone.

"I do," Aaron said. "I'm going to take Mia home and make passionate love to her."

Everyone burst out laughing as Mia punched Aaron in the arm. She turned ten shades of red and choked on her wine. "Aaron, my God, I'm going to kill you right now."

Tuesday night was good. Wine, beer, and food filled their bellies as the celebration continued. Everyone hugged, laughed, and stated their appreciation for good food, good fortune and good friends.

"Vic, this is what life is all about. Pretty soon Max will join us again. We're friends for life... all of us. We're family. Don't ever forget that." Mia hugged Vic. Everyone embraced each other, expressed their love, and went home to get some sleep.

Chapter Twenty-Four

The friends went to Peekskill on Saturday as a group. They took two cars and decided to make a day of it. Max was allowed visitors for two hours a day, nothing more, per doctor's orders, and could only have three visitors at a time. The doctor didn't want Max to get overstimulated. Lunch was planned for afterward, then shopping in Beacon, Mia's favorite small town, with antique stores and galleries lining the streets.

The doctor gathered them together in the fourth-floor family center. "Max is doing exceptionally well. His brain-function tests show remarkable improvement. He's on the mend and will be released in a few days. He'll need to come here for therapy three times a week, or the therapist can go to his home. Max can't be left alone. Someone has to be with him until his broken legs heal and he can walk. Where does his family live, and why hasn't a relative come to visit him?"

Everyone stared blankly at the doctor. There were no words. They'd never met Max's family or even heard stories about them. Being the only person in the room with information about anything—and that was the motorcycle-club story—Mia wasn't about to open her mouth. No way on God's earth would she spill that to anyone. Aaron would wonder why she had knowledge about Max when Vic didn't. It wouldn't add up, so the truth would remain hidden. But somebody had to say something.

"Max can come home with me," Vic said. "My brother is staying at my house temporarily, and I can take time off work. It will be fine. We'll make him comfortable."

"Very well, then. You'll have to sign the medical power of attorney papers when he's released. That's only if Max is coherent enough to understand what's going on. He has to agree to stay at your home, Ms. Alonso. We'll locate some therapists that do home-care visits and get it set up." The doctor shook everyone's hand and left to do his Saturday morning rounds.

They went in to visit, a few at a time. Max recognized everyone, and he appeared happy to see them. He was confused about a few names, but the doctor said that might happen.

"Don't worry, Max. It will all come back soon," Vic said.

They stayed for two hours, taking turns at his bedside and talking to him. Max dozed off occasionally during the visit. They didn't want to exhaust him, so they said goodbyes and left for the day. Mario and Vic made plans to return on Tuesday to check Max out of the hospital.

***

Mia, Tina, and Sasha helped at Vic's house Sunday night. Furniture had to be repositioned to accommodate a wheelchair passing through. Vic set up the third bedroom, currently used as her office, as Max's new quarters. The desk was put in the garage for the time being, and Vic moved her laptop to the dining room table. She hoped Max would be okay with the arrangement.

"How am I going to help him with his personal stuff?" Vic asked as they sat down to take a break.

"The therapists will be here part of the time," Sasha said.

"Yeah, but they aren't nurses, and that isn't their job. They're physical and occupational therapists. He can't take a bath or shower, and he's way too heavy for me to move around. Do I give him sponge baths? Will he be able to go to the bathroom alone?"

"Vic, you need to ask the doctor those questions. I'm sure Max wouldn't mind sponge baths from you though. Maybe a little stimulation will help him recover faster." Tina gave her a wink.

"Tina, I swear you're going to hell. You're an evil woman. I'll worry about Max becoming stimulated when he's in better shape. I'm not going to take advantage of him."

"Since when haven't you taken advantage of a good opportunity when you had the chance? Banged up or not, Max Cole is one hunk of a guy. He's drop-dead gorgeous and sexier than shit. I'm just saying…"

Vic and Mario made last-minute adjustments in the house Tuesday morning before they left to pick up Max. Vic felt excited but anxious.

"Mario, am I doing the right thing, bringing Max back home with me?"

"Well, Sis, I don't know him yet, but from the look of things, you have serious feelings for Max. Do what's in your heart. In a few days, you'll be on your own with him. It's a big responsibility taking care of someone and working at the same time. The last thing you want to do is become stressed and delay his recovery. You have to be comfortable with each other in this situation. It isn't the easiest way to start a relationship."

"You're such a smart and insightful brother. I love you, and I'm so happy you're back in New York. Max should be walking in ten days. The doctor is going to fit him with leg braces, and he has crutches already. That alone will take pressure off me. Otherwise, it's really just the therapies he has to work on. He'll be as good as new in a few months. I want to pick up where we were before this happened. He is a wonderful person. I don't know the whole story behind the man. We haven't gotten that far yet, but I believe in him. I believe in us."

"Then that's what you need to focus on, Sis. I want you to be happy. If Max is who does it for you, then go for it. You have to give it your very best effort. Let's see how it goes for the next few days. I'll feel a lot better leaving you alone to take care of him if it looks doable."

"Yeah, and don't forget, I have friends that are concerned about Max, too. All it takes is a phone call."

"That's what friends are for, and you have the best bunch anyone could ask for. I'm glad you stayed in Tarrytown. If down the road Max and I do become partners in business, I'll be here often, and I like that idea."

"Me too. Well… we're here. Let's take Max home."

***

Max's condition improved each and every day. His speech and motor skills were almost back to normal from the constant exercises with the therapists. Max and Vic often sat on the edge of his twin bed and talked. The room was small and sparsely decorated with a bed, a dresser with a TV perched on top of it, and a small nightstand. The lighting was dim with only that small table next to the bed. It held the solitary lamp in the room. Vic made sure they spent a few hours every night after dinner talking about the past, and very little about the present or future. Max needed speech therapy every day, and by talking, they learned more about each other's youth. Max had had a rough childhood, but so had Vic. They had that in common. He told her bits and pieces about the motorcycle gang he used to run with. Max wasn't quite ready to confess all his transgressions. The timing wasn't right. He told Vic how being in the gang had made him lose touch with his family. His family gave him an ultimatum, and at that time, he chose the gang. He hadn't seen his parents or siblings in years.

"Why don't you reconnect with them? Family is everything." Vic handed him a cold beer as they sat on the deck in her large backyard. Max used the wheelchair but made an effort to stand for short periods of time every day with a cane for support.

"It's complicated. I tried to reconnect with them once years ago, but it didn't go over well. I guess riding up to their house on my Harley still sent the wrong message. They're old school. My siblings were young then and very impressionable. Anyway, they all moved to Pennsylvania in 1995, and I haven't seen them since. How about you— what's your story?"

"I grew up here for most of my life. I was born in the Bronx, where my cousins are." She gave Max a quick smile as they reminisced about her cousin's wedding. "I can't complain too much about my childhood other than that I was the only girl and we didn't have much. I guess we were poor. We're proud Puerto Ricans though. My dad never asked for handouts, and he worked several jobs to make ends meet. My mom was a homemaker. With my crazy brothers and cousins around all the time, she had to stay home to keep the place in one piece."

They laughed. Vic thought about her youth, and when Max was quiet, she was pretty sure he was lost in his own personal memories, both good and bad.

"Growing up in the Bronx was tough, at least that's what my folks said. I guess anywhere in the city was scary for parents, wondering if their kids got to school safely every day. Anyway, by the time I started primary school, we'd moved to Tarrytown. It's the only place I can remember living. I love it here. I wouldn't want to live anywhere else. Do you like living in Peekskill?"

"Nah… it doesn't hold special memories of my childhood or anything. I stayed in Peekskill because I began working as a wilderness guide. That's when I finally got my head on straight, thirteen years ago. The location was convenient, nothing more."

"Are you hungry? I can get lunch started. How about a BLT?"

"That sounds great."

Max reached for Vic's hand as she got up to go into the kitchen. She paused, letting her hand rest in his, and looked deep into his eyes. The feelings were there. Their eyes didn't lie, yet their lips couldn't speak the truth. Vic had doubts and insecurities she couldn't share with him.

"Vic?"

"Yes, Max?"

"We need to discuss how long I'm going to stay here. I'll be walking in a week. As soon as I get fitted with braces, I'll be able to do everything on my own. It's been two weeks already, and I don't want to put you out. It's almost time for me to go home. You have a business to run, and there isn't much I can do around here to earn my keep. I'm a proud man, Vic."

The smile that crossed Max's lips was enough to send Vic over the edge. She wanted to kiss him and make love with him. He was in her mind and dreams every minute.

The place Max needed to be was in her bed.

She caught her breath and let it out slowly. She wanted this man more than she'd ever wanted anything in her life, but there were obstacles. Max had no idea Vic knew about his whirlwind affair with Mia. No one had told him how Vic had seen him and Mia together in the driveway the night of the party. The guilt and insecurity that tore at Vic's heart were eating away at her. She wanted to make things right. She wanted to confess to Max and come clean about everything she knew and saw, but she was afraid because she blamed herself for Max's accident and was afraid he did, too.

And bringing up the subject of his intimacy with Mia was impossible. Sure, Mia had known him first, and what they'd done together had nothing to do with Vic. Nobody had betrayed her. But the embarrassment Max might feel if Vic admitted she knew could be enough to send him packing for good and ruin the trust between them. So, instead of coming closer, she started pulling away.

Chapter Twenty-Five

Sasha sat at the conference table, fidgeting with the pen in her hand. The owners of the Victorian chose this downtown bank as the place to do the closing. She wanted to get it over with and have those keys in her hand. Her apartment in Manhattan had sold a few weeks earlier, and the closing had already taken place. She felt good about ending that chapter of her life and moving on. Tarrytown was a new city, a new atmosphere, where the old Sasha had no place, but the new Sasha would thrive. She'd fallen in love with Tarrytown months ago, and now she was falling in love all over again with the Victorian. Every room was already painted and decorated in her mind. She'd started a scrapbook the month before, ripping pages out of *Better Homes and Gardens* magazine. Sasha had known the Victorian would be hers six weeks ago. She was a woman on a mission, and nobody was about to get in her way. She signed the papers and handed over the check for the agreed-upon price.

The Victorian is mine! Just give me the damn keys so I can get out of here. I want to be in my house. Patience wasn't

Sasha's greatest virtue, but even so, she had to go through the motions, legalities, and explanations. At last, the keys were dropped into her waiting hand. She thanked the bankers and previous owners then bolted out the door. Josh Redmond waited, curbside, in his car to take her home.

"Josh, you really got me the Victorian. I can't believe it. I need to pinch myself to see if it's real." Sasha already had the door open, ready to jump out of the car, before Josh had come to a complete stop in the driveway.

"Slow down, Sasha, you're going to hurt yourself," he said, laughing.

"Sorry... do you want to come in for a minute?" She couldn't suppress her joy and happiness. She hadn't been in the house in three weeks. It was like seeing it again for the first time. She ran through each room, squealing with excitement and plotting the color palette for the formal rooms. She could feel Josh's eyes on her, probably sizing her up as a trophy. She'd once seen herself in that light, too, but since moving to Tarrytown, she was just Sasha. That was the way she liked it.

***

Josh watched Sasha, focused on her beauty. Any man would covet her. She was arm candy and a masterpiece finer than the *Mona Lisa*. "Hey, Sasha, let me take you out for lunch as a celebration of the closing. You pick the place—my treat." He followed her from room to room, waiting for an answer.

"Um… okay, sure, but I don't want to be gone too long. I have so many ideas in my head. I need to get back here and start writing things down. I have to buy a car, too. I can't keep expecting people to drive me around now that I'll be buying paint and supplies all the time."

"I'd be happy to take you on errands," Josh said too enthusiastically.

"Why would you do that?" she asked, stopping in her tracks.

"Well, just to be neighborly, I guess." Saying he wanted to be neighborly was a neutral comment, safe and noncommittal. Josh needed to dial it back before Sasha became suspicious of his intentions. He didn't want to appear too eager and come across as pathetic. But she was too beautiful to let slip between his fingers. He needed to get her attention, but at the moment, it seemed hopeless. The Victorian took center stage. *Maybe in a few weeks I'll try harder. The newness of the house might wear off by then. I wonder what she's heard about me from Mia, Tina, and Vic. Whatever it is, it can't be good. I need to be on my best behavior and act like a gentleman if I ever want a chance with her.*

***

With lunch over and Sasha happily back in the home of her dreams, she said good-bye to Josh and went inside. She had a to-do list a mile long. She sat on the hardwood floor, scanning each room and the wide-open spaces. She looked down the long, once-elegant hallway that led to the ornate double front doors with beveled glass. Visions of days gone by and high-society parties filled her mind. *I'll have parties and lots of them. They'll write about the beautiful Victorian in the local society pages. It will be a showplace. People will flock to Sunrise Avenue just to see the Victorian and take pictures of its beauty. And it's all mine.* Sasha smiled from ear to ear as she gently rubbed the faded maple floor next to her. *If these floors could talk. Don't worry—pretty soon you're going to glisten like new.*

Sasha needed help. It was time to call in the troops. She grabbed the bottle of water off the deep windowsill and went outside to sit on the porch. The cell reception in the house was poor at best, likely because of the many rooms with little nooks and crannies.

***

"Mia, it's Sasha. Are you busy today?"

"Nope. What's up?" Mia configured the Bluetooth around her ear. She needed both hands for slicing tomatoes and cheese. Today, a club sandwich was her lunch. She layered the turkey, cheese and tomatoes between slices of wheat bread as she listened to Sasha speed talk.

"I had the closing on the Victorian this morning. I'm there now. Will you come by and help me with my to-do list and throw ideas at me? There's something else I need to do too."

"What's that?" Mia asked with a chuckle. She enjoyed this new and improved version of Sasha.

"Well… are there any honest used-car dealers in town? You know, somebody that won't rip me off?"

"Sure. Tim Murray is pretty honest, but you actually want to buy a car?" Mia laughed. "Have you ever driven a car in your life?"

"Well, no, but I'm sure somebody will teach me. Anyway, I don't want a car—I want a truck," Sasha announced proudly.

Mia burst out laughing and continued until tears rolled down her cheeks. "Girl, I'm starting to love you more every day. You aren't the Sasha I met months ago. Who are you, and what have you done with the prissy little Manhattan model I used to know and hate?"

Sasha giggled. "I turned into one of your best friends. You can never have too many best friends, right, sister?"

"That's right, hon. I'll be there in ten minutes. Do you want a sandwich?"

"No, thanks. Josh Redmond took me out for lunch. I'll take a bottle of water though."

"Okay. You can tell me all about adorable Josh when I get there. Out."

***

Max practiced his steps every day while Vic was at work, and he was becoming stronger on his feet. He did his cumbersome walking exercises outside on the deck where there was more room to maneuver. He was using crutches, but his appointment to be fitted with leg braces was the next day. Max was far from 100 percent recovered, but with the braces, he'd be able to walk until he got tired. Tomorrow would be the day he'd leave Tarrytown and return home. He and Vic hadn't progressed in the last few weeks the way he hoped. Something didn't feel right, and he had no idea why. Vic had a nurturing way about her, but she shut down whenever Max talked about becoming a real couple.

He sat at the table on the deck, tired of the daily exercises. Max carried Vic's cordless house phone in his pocket and called his buddy and scout counselor, Gary Miller. They'd spoken right after Max got out of the hospital. Gary had told him to call back as soon as he could walk without assistance. He suggested that Max ought to consider working as a lecturer at different Boy Scout camps for the time being. Max had a long recovery ahead of him before he would be capable of going out on wilderness hikes. Any opportunity to get back outdoors with the Scouts was something Max needed to take—he was chomping at the bit. Sitting around most of the time in a wheelchair drove him crazy. Tomorrow, he would walk without assistance. Max needed to get back to what he loved: being in nature.

Vic pulled into the driveway at five fifteen. Max sat on the front porch, waiting, with two cold beers. He smiled at the sight of her. He was a man in love, but he was also a realist. If Vic didn't want to pursue a relationship with him, it would be time to cut ties. Max would go back to Peekskill, back to his solitary life, and spend his days with the Boy Scouts and nature. He'd lived that life before Vic and enjoyed it. It would be heartbreaking, but he'd do it again if she gave him no other choice.

"Hi, gorgeous," he said, reaching out to hand her a glass of beer. "How was your day?"

"Okay. The same old thing, but that's business. Tomorrow will be exciting, right?" She reached for the beer and took a sip.

"You mean because of the braces?" Max punched through the foam and took a gulp of the Java Head Stout.

"Yeah… you're happy, aren't you?"

"Sure I am, but we need to talk about that. Do you want to stay out here or go inside?"

She gave Max a look that said, "I don't want to hear what you're going to tell me." It was a look of dread.

"I guess we can stay outside. It's a beautiful day." Vic stared down at the steps. She didn't make eye contact with Max. She took another sip of beer and looked west, toward the end of the street, facing away from him.

"Vic, I'm going home tomorrow after I get the braces fitted on my legs. I've got to deal with the insurance company about my Harley and make sure my health insurance is taking care of the hospital bills. My mail has been held for three weeks, and I'm sure there are bills piling up." Max laughed nervously. "Anyway, there's no reason to stay here and have you wait on me hand and foot. It isn't fair to you, and I'll be fine on my own. I talked to Gary Miller earlier. He's the scout counselor I've known for years. He's pretty sure I can work part-time lecturing kids about safety in the woods and teamwork on overnight hikes. It will do me good to get back to work. I've missed it."

"I'll miss you, Max."

"I'm glad you understand, Vic. I guess you can drop me off at my house after the doctor's visit. It's probably the easiest way to do this. I still have my truck, thankfully. I need to practice driving to see if my legs work right. If not, Gary can pick me up for work until I'm completely healed. He only lives five miles from me."

Vic was silent. Max reached for her hand, but she abruptly pulled it away and went into the house. He sat on the step, alone with his beer and his thoughts. Max loved Vic, but he didn't know how to break through the invisible wall that was separating them. He didn't understand it, and she wouldn't open up.

Chapter Twenty-Six

Max's doctor's appointment was at eleven o'clock. He woke to the sound of coffee beans grinding in the kitchen. By the delicious scent wafting through the air and down the hallway, it was likely bacon would be served with breakfast. He rolled over carefully. The clock read 7:13 a.m.

How did everything get so screwed up? I was sure Vic wanted me to stay. I thought we were on the right track. Now, it's like we've lost everything we had. We're strangers again. Why can't we eat breakfast, drink coffee, and laugh together? I want to kiss her good morning and make love to her later. What went wrong?

He got up, showered, and dressed. He felt awkward and wanted to get the day over with. The few items of clothing he had with him were packed in five minutes. He set the army-green duffel bag near the front door and walked into the kitchen.

Vic popped four slices of wheat bread into the toaster. Two plates sat on the counter, ready for heaping spoonsful of scrambled eggs to fill the empty surfaces. She turned and said good morning to Max. "There's a pot of fresh coffee on the table. Help yourself."

"Thanks. It sure smells good in here... Vic?"

"Sit down and eat your food so it doesn't get cold." She plopped eggs, bacon, and toast on each plate and carried them to the table where Max had sat for meals during the last three weeks. She seated herself in the chair to his right and began eating without another word.

Max's appointment was at the Peekskill Medical Clinic, next door to the hospital, with Doctor Farrow, the orthopedist. He would be Max's primary doctor for the braces and anything related to his legs. The appointment lasted two hours between X-rays, fitting the braces, and Max's questions. In between each procedure, Max sat in the waiting room with Vic. He felt uncomfortable. They were in love but stuck, and they didn't know how to move forward. The medical clinic wasn't the right place to talk, and from Vic's reaction the night before, Max felt certain she didn't want to talk anyway.

***

Vic helped him carry the crutches and duffel bag to his front door. Max walked stiffly with the new braces on his legs. It would take time getting used to them.

"Well, I guess this is it." He pulled out his house keys and fumbled with the deadbolt. "Vic... can I at least hug you? You've done so much for me these last few weeks. I really appreciate you. Please take care of yourself. Tell everyone thanks for helping out. I plan to get a new phone this week, and I'd like to keep in touch." Max put his arms around her and embraced her. She didn't resist, but she didn't respond, either.

"Good-bye, Max. Take care. I hope you recover quickly so you can get back to what you love the most… the kids."

Her words stung his heart and soul. She was what he loved the most. He knew that she knew it, but for whatever reason, she'd given up on them. As though surprised at the harsh words she'd spoken, Vic grimaced as she turned and walked back to her car. She drove away without waving or looking back.

Max walked into his house. The quiet and darkness tore at his heart. He longed for the sound of Vic's laugh. He would miss her quick wit and the fluent sarcasm and that cocky Puerto Rican dialect. Most of all, he would miss her beauty. Her inner and outer beauty took his breath away every time he looked at her. He sat alone, pounding the kitchen table with his fist, and cried.

***

A block down the street, Vic pulled over and killed the engine. She sobbed into her hands as her body wretched with anguish. Her heart ached more than it ever had before.

***

Classic rock blasted from the radio in Mia's car Wednesday morning as she honked the horn in front of

Tina's house. Sasha bounded out, wearing a tiny, tight tank top and cut-off shorts. Those red rhinestone sandals from days gone by adorned her beautifully pedicured feet. The nail polish in a bright, firehouse red glistened on each toenail. Her hair, piled on top of her head in a sexy, jumbled-up mess, looked stunning. Sasha was a hottie even when she didn't try to be. The look she wore had probably taken five minutes to put together.

Damn it, girl! You're gorgeous no matter what you do. Mia shook her head and laughed. "Are you ready to rock and roll, babe?" she asked as Sasha jumped into the passenger seat. Mia was prepared for what came next.

"Ouch… son of a bitch. These black seats will be the death of me."

"It's the short shorts that will be the death of you, or maybe the death of any breathing male in Tarrytown. Reach into the backseat. I brought a towel for you to sit on. I'll keep it in the car from now on or at least until winter when you start wearing pants."

Sasha giggled. "Thanks, Mia. I'm so excited for today. I'm going to get a truck. Yippee!"

"You're friggin' insane. Why do you want a used truck anyway? You can afford something brand-new."

"I'm being smart and frugal. Think about it: the money I save on a vehicle can go toward home repairs. How responsible is that?"

"Good job, hon. I'm impressed. Let's see what Tim has on the used car lot. By the way you're dressed today, he'll try to sell you everything under the sun, including sand in the desert, just to keep you there."

"I don't get it," Sasha said, looking totally confused.

"Never mind, you goof. It was a compliment. So, if we find what you're looking for, Aaron agreed to teach you how to drive as long as I videotape it." Mia laughed.

"You guys are going to have fun at my expense, aren't you?"

"Damn straight. I wouldn't miss that for anything."

They arrived at Murray's Auto Mall at ten in the morning. Mia had called the day before to let Tim know they were coming. She wanted to get the best deal for Sasha, and that would come from the owner himself. Mia had known Tim most of her life. She also did all the photography for his ad campaigns in the newspaper. He owed her a favor. Being around Sasha wasn't a favor in men's eyes, though—it was a godsend. The dealership, on the edge of town, was at the corner of two busy intersections. Tim did well, and his was one of the most successful car lots in the area. He'd told Mia there were four used trucks in the lot and that he'd meet them on the used-car side when they arrived.

Mia pulled around to the south side of the dealership. A small building with the words "Used Cars," in green neon lights, sat in the lot next to the various cars and trucks.

"I see the trucks!" Sasha yelled out enthusiastically when Mia found a place to park.

Tim Murray walked out of the building and stared at Sasha like a hungry dog ready to pounce on a T-bone steak. "Hello, Mia. And who do we have here?" He smiled like a Cheshire cat at the sight of the dark-haired goddess walking toward him.

"Hi, I'm Sasha Renaud, and I want to buy a truck, please," she said with more than enough enthusiasm for the three of them.

"Nice to meet you, Sasha," Tim said, giving Mia an approving raise of the eyebrows. "Is there anything special you're looking for in a truck?"

"Yes. I want a radio. What color trucks do you have?"

"Okay, then," he responded, looking a little dumbfounded.

Mia giggled under her breath at his expression.

"Well... we have silver, black, green, and red. They all have different features though."

"I want the red one," Sasha said with as much excitement as if she were shopping on Madison Avenue.

"Okay, just follow me. Here it is." Tim read out the window information sticker. "Let's see... it's a 2007 Toyota Tundra. There's a radio, CD player, air conditioning, automatic transmission, four-wheel drive, cloth bucket seats, and fifty-seven thousand miles on it. It's gone through our safety inspection, so it has a clean bill of health." Tim laughed at his own clever comment.

"How much is it?" Sasha asked, not having the slightest idea what trucks cost.

Mia gave Tim a stern look as a reminder of their long-term friendship.

"Well, the sticker price is $23,500 because of the low

miles, but we can do a little better than that for you. A friend of Mia's is a friend of ours. Let's go inside and talk this over. Can I get you two something to drink?"

"Thank you—I'll have a Perrier," Sasha said. Mia elbowed her in the side. "I mean, a Diet Coke is fine."

"I'll have the same, Tim. Thanks."

He disappeared around the corner. Mia heard him rifling through the mini-fridge on the other side of the wall.

"What do you think of the truck? It's pretty, isn't it?" Sasha asked.

"Yes, it's pretty. Let's see if he gives you a pretty price. Let me do the talking, okay?"

"Got it. Thanks."

Tim returned with three icy cans of Diet Coke. "Well, I checked with our used-car manager, and he thinks we have a little room to play. I can sell you that truck today for $21,750. How does that sound?" he asked, with a wide, toothy grin.

"That sounds like shit," Mia responded.

"Mia!" Sasha said, startled. "I like the truck."

"We want to take the truck home for the night. I'll have Aaron check it out, and I'll get back to you tomorrow. My car will stay here, so you don't have to worry about anything. Bottom line," Mia said as she stood up, "is not a penny over $19,500. Now, we've got things to do, so cough up the keys."

"Okay, Mia. Man, you're a tough one. I'll talk to you tomorrow. Enjoy the truck, Sasha."

"Oh, I will. Thank you."

Mia and Sasha hopped in the truck and drove off. Sasha bounced up and down with glee.

"I'm not even burning my legs on the seats because they're cloth. I'm so happy. Do you think I'll get the truck?"

"Of course you will, honey. Let's go to Home Depot and get some of the stuff on your list. We have an entire truck bed to fill up."

The girls bought dozens of outlet and light-switch covers. They picked out a beautiful dining-room-ceiling fixture. It was elegant, fitting in with the era of the Victorian. Three more ceiling fixtures for the bedrooms were purchased with fans attached. A garbage disposal, brooms, mops, buckets, garbage cans, and cleaning products filled the back of the truck.

"I guess you were right," Mia said.

"About what?"

"A truck is a handy vehicle to have. Good job, girl. We'll drop this stuff off at the house and grab some lunch. Let's see if Tina and Vic want to join us."

"That sounds like fun. Can we go to Morey's?"

"Sure, no prob. After lunch, we'll make some calls. You already started a list of repairs that are needed right?"

"Yep, starting with the roof and outside painting. Let's talk about colors during lunch. Vic and Tina can give me ideas, too."

Chapter Twenty-Seven

The girls walked from Hair Brained to Morey's at noon. The sky was the bluest blue, not a cloud to interrupt the flawless palette of brilliance.

Sasha stared up at the sky as they walked. "What about shades of blue for the Victorian?"

"Tina hates blue, so don't ask her," Vic growled.

"Who said I hate blue?"

"I don't know. I'm in a bitchy mood, so you're the designated patsy for the day."

"Well, that's a bunch of shit. Anyway, Sasha, let's check out some painted ladies on Google images when we get to Morey's. There are so many gorgeous colors that would fit in with your new neighborhood. You know, more natural colors like pale greens, corals and mustards."

"Blue isn't natural? The sky and the ocean are blue," Sasha said, confused again.

Mia interjected, "Let's decide over a beer, okay?"

"Sure," Sasha said. "Anyway, how do you like my new truck? Pretty sweet ride, huh?"

"I like it," Tina agreed.

"Vic, what do you think?"

"Who cares? It's a friggin' truck."

Sasha began crying and marched ahead to Morey's alone.

"Do you have PMS or something today? Damn it, Vic, give the girl a break. She's really excited about life," Mia said, trying to keep order.

"No shit, Vic. Take it down a notch. What's up your ass anyway?" Tina snarled.

"I'm pissed, okay? Max moved back home, but you're well aware of that. I just let the best man I've ever known leave me, and I didn't do a damn thing to stop him." Now Vic was crying.

"Oh my friggin' God, now we have two crybabies," Mia said as they entered the front door of Morey's. Sasha was sitting alone in a booth, looking like a sad little puppy. Vic looked as if she wanted to kill anyone who talked to her. "Tina, you sit next to Sasha. I'll sit next to Vic. If anyone starts something, we'll give them a swift punch to the arm."

"Great advice, but don't you think Vic will just hit back twice as hard?" Tina asked apprehensively.

"Whatever... let's order our drinks. Morey we need two pitchers of beer to start."

"Coming right up, Mia. Just give me a minute," he shouted back.

"Okay, here's kind of what I mean." Tina showed Sasha the Ferndale, California website on Google images. "I love this town. It has the best Victorians I've ever seen.

Look at the Gingerbread Inn. These are the colors I was trying to describe to you. Don't you think they're beautiful? See how nicely they blend in with nature? They're soft and subtle. The colors aren't a stark contrast to earth tones, like blue would be. I don't have anything against blue, I'm just saying… that's all."

Sasha gasped. "Do you think the Victorian could be this beautiful?"

"Of course she can," Tina said. "She already is. She needs love and attention, that's all."

"You called the Victorian a *she*," Sasha said. "How come?"

"Anything beautiful is a she. An airplane, a ship, the Victorian—each one is a she."

"I love that! *She* is going to have the exact colors as the Gingerbread Inn. She's almost the same style, with the beautiful turret and spindles everywhere. There, it's settled. The Victorian, I mean, *she*, will be painted light mustard and coral with dark-blue window trim. The roof will have charcoal-gray shingles just like in the picture. Now, I need to hire a painter and a roofer. Mia, will you help me pick out someone?"

"Of course, Sasha. Why don't we go ahead and order lunch? We'll work on that later."

Mia stared at Vic, worried. As though sensing Mia's worry, Vic glanced up and looked her way. She raised her eyebrows at Vic as if to say, "We'll talk later, okay?"

Vic gave an affirmative nod and calmed down enough to apologize to Tina and Sasha for her earlier behavior.

"I'm sorry, guys. I'm going through an emotional stage. I'll be fine sooner or later."

Mia texted Vic under the table, saying she couldn't meet with her that night, but she could the next day. She would connect with Vic at Bottoms Up after work. Vic looked down at her phone and then nodded. Tina and Sasha were too busy to notice. They were head to head, elbows on the table, talking full speed about interior house colors.

***

Aaron joined Mia and Sasha at the Victorian right after he closed the camera shop for the day. It was six thirty, and they'd already made pretty good progress with the cleaning. Earlier, they'd brought over a few items from Tina's house in the Tundra—of course, with Mia behind the wheel. Tina loaned Sasha a card table and chairs. The table worked fine as a planning area and a place to relax and have lunch.

"This house is going to be a masterpiece when it's done," Aaron said, envisioning what the completion would look like. He could tell already that Sasha was all in, but no matter what, the Victorian would be one of the most beautiful homes in Tarrytown. He gave Mia a passionate kiss on the lips and Sasha a peck on the cheek. "Yuck… you guys are all salty and sweaty." He grimaced and groaned as he wiped off his mouth.

"Thanks a lot. You know a woman's work is never done, or so they say," Mia responded with a raised eyebrow.

"Yeah, and I bet it was a man that made up that stupid phrase," Sasha added. "Do you want to check out my cool ride, Aaron?"

"Sure. From the street it looks pretty clean. Let's take a look." They walked single file out the front door and to the driveway. Everyone inhaled the cooler temperature and welcome breeze. The old windows, which were painted closed, didn't afford them much circulation indoors.

Aaron crawled under the truck, poked and prodded, then checked under the hood. No leaks anywhere. No rust or anything that rattled when he took it out for a test-drive either. "So, are you ready?"

"Ready for what?" Sasha asked when he returned.

"Well… are you going to hire a driver, or are you going to learn how to drive this beast yourself?" Aaron asked.

"Yay, I'm going to learn how to drive. Right here, right now?"

"Yep, let's go."

The three piled into the truck with Aaron behind the wheel. Sasha sat in the passenger seat, watching closely. Mia sat in the jump seat behind her. Aaron drove to an abandoned factory on the edge of town, which had an enormous parking lot.

"This will do just fine." He climbed out of the truck. "Sasha, front and center."

Sasha remained seated and looked back at Mia with questioning eyes.

"That means get out and go around to the driver's side," Mia instructed her.

"Oh... okay." She walked around the truck, grabbed the handle on the upper part of the door, stepped on the running board, and pulled herself into the driver's seat. She giggled as she sat proudly behind the steering wheel. Aaron got in on the passenger's side.

"Now, adjust the mirrors so you can see everything behind you. Adjust the seat, too, so it's comfortable for you. You need to be able to reach the gas and the brake pedals without any effort. It has to feel natural."

"Okay, I'm ready."

"All right, you have a shifter here. The selections you'll use most of the time are park, reverse, and drive. The other shifter is for the four-wheel drive, which you don't have to worry about right now. The gas is on your right, and the brake is on your left. Hold down the brake, shift out of park, and put the truck in drive. Don't touch the gas pedal until I tell you to, and then barely press it with your foot. Put your seat belt on first."

Sasha was giggling again, probably from nerves. She kept her foot on the brake as she shifted into drive. She gradually moved her foot to the gas pedal and pressed it. The truck lurched forward. Sasha screamed. Mia burst out laughing and almost dropped her cell phone while she was videotaping. "This is going to take a while," she said as she hiccupped from laughing so hard.

Chapter Twenty-Eight

With Mia and Karen joining her, Sasha returned the following day to Tim Murray's Auto Mall and purchased the truck.

"You drive a hard bargain, Mia," Tim teased. In his opinion, keeping friends and business associates happy made good sense, especially when living in a close-knit community like Tarrytown.

Over the course of the next week, Sasha got the hang of driving. She drove often but always with Mia as her sidekick. Sasha hadn't taken the driver's test for her actual license yet, so she drove on a learner's permit. Mia let her try driving the Camaro several times, but getting the hang of a stick shift proved too much for Sasha to grasp, at least for the time being.

The contractors were hired for the roof and the exterior painting. Sasha's focus was on the outer appearances and weatherproofing first. The electrical and plumbing repairs would begin after the exterior was complete. The interior could be done room by room until everything looked perfect. New York's long, cold winters were just months away and would give Sasha the perfect reason to stay inside, cozy up with a roaring fire and a cup of cocoa, and start painting walls. She pictured painting parties she would host. They'd have catered lunches and plenty of Merlot. Sasha not only envisioned the Victorian as her beloved home but as everyone's home, a place they'd all taken part in finding and would nurture back to health together. Her friends were all on board to lend a helping hand. Soon, the house that Sasha had fallen madly in love with would come alive as a renewed masterpiece. She would return to her original glory, the way she'd stood proudly over a century ago.

***

Vic sat alone as she had a lot lately. The house was quiet, and the lights were dim. She wasn't the bubbly Puerto Rican hot mama she portrayed every day at Hair Brained. That was her professional and public persona. Everyone expected it of her—the crazy, loud, boisterous, funny woman who had over fifty personal clients. They were as loyal and protective of her as a mother would be to her child. Anyone who got between Vic and her clients would have hell to pay. The culprit would go down in a burst of flames. The old blue hairs, as well as the young hipsters, all booked their appointments months in advance so they were guaranteed to be at Vic's chair. Nobody else would do. Vic wore many hats, and everyone loved her. She was their hairdresser, confidant, mother, daughter, and comedian for two hours every single month.

Tonight, she was lonely, like last night and the nights to come. Her heart broke for Max. She hadn't spoken to him since the day he got fitted for his leg braces. They'd parted ways on his doorstep with a hug and nothing more. There were no expectations, no future dates planned, and no promises made.

The wine rack filled with bottles of Merlot mocked her from the kitchen. It beckoned her to come and partake of the grape. She stared at the bottles until they won. "Why the hell not? Tomorrow is Tuesday—I don't have to work anyway." She grabbed a bottle and pulled the corkscrew out of the top left utensil drawer. The metallic seal over the cork was sliced off with the tiny knife and a quick twist of her wrist. The corkscrew sank deep into the cork with each turn. She pulled it out with a pop. The wineglass waited, anticipating the dark grape nectar of the gods to be poured into it. Vic drank and enjoyed it—over and over again.

She sat and blankly stared at the TV. The bottles of wine sat side by side on the coffee table just in case. Her phone rang out from deep within the front pocket of her Lucky jeans. *Such irony.* She pulled out the cell. The caller ID showed that her sweet brother Mario needed to talk to her.

"Hey, Sis, how's it hanging?"

"Isn't that what a girl says to a guy?" she asked.

"Funny. Anyway, I wanted to give you a heads-up. I'm meeting with Max tomorrow to go over business ideas for the Peekskill area. He's going to show me around. I guess there are a few vacant buildings in prime locations downtown that might be perfect. Good exposure and decent storefronts, so he says. We've talked a lot since he's been home. Something seems to be distracting him, like his mind isn't focused on our conversations. Do you know why?"

"C'mon, Mario, stop torturing me like that." Vic turned down the TV and filled her glass. "It's complicated."

"Well... uncomplicate it. I need him to be on board and focused if I plan to partner up with him. Peekskill isn't a good location for skiing, but there's plenty of hiking, camping, and mountain biking in the area. Outdoor-sports gear is hot. It would be a super business to own. We'll have skiing in Hunter and everything else in Peekskill. So, tell me what's going on with the two of you."

"I'm insecure. Max is way too handsome for the likes of me. There are tons of women better suited for him."

"Really? That's why he's single, right? He wants to be with you, and you're pushing him away because you're insecure? You need a head check, Sis. Believe it or not, Max is in love with you. I want you to fix things with him so we can get our new business venture off the ground. I'll tell him you miss him. Talk to you."

"Mario, don't you dare!"

"Can't hear you—bad connection."

Damn you, Mario. Now I'm going to seem desperate. Vic groaned and grabbed the remote. She channel surfed up and down the list, finally stopping on Nat Geo's episode on Human Behavior. *This sounds interesting. Apparently, our basic behaviors are the same as a pack of dogs. Awesome. That sounds about as pathetic as me.* She reached for the second bottle of Merlot and cozied up in the recliner, pouring another glass.

Vic woke with the sun trying to laser cut a beam through her eyelids. "Son of a bitch—that's bright," she growled. It was more than clear that she'd woken up on the wrong side of the recliner and had a raging hangover. Her feet weighed a ton as she shuffled toward the kitchen. Alka Seltzer was calling her name. "Plop, plop, fizz, fizz… and whatever," she grumbled, as she held a glass under the tap and filled it half-full of water. Two white tablets were dropped in, and the distinct fizzing sound bubbled in the glass. Vic chugged it and gagged but kept it down. *That'll teach me… Ms. Pathetic.*

***

The insurance adjuster thanked Max for his time and drove away. They met at the local garage where the tow truck had brought Max's Harley. Shock spread across his face when he saw the tangled pile of metal that used to be his prized customized bike. Both tires were blown out, and the rims were destroyed. Strange how the chrome still glistened in the sun even with scrapes and mud and grass lodged in every cavity. The beautiful painted mural of a forest scene on the gas tank was reduced to crushed metal scored with dents the size of softballs. The twisted handlebars resembled a giant Bavarian pretzel, and the handmade saddlebags were nothing but shreds of leather. He hung his head, thanking God for his life, but sad none-the-less. The bike could be replaced, but what about Vic? Had she lost interest because of his injuries? Max was about seventy-five percent back to normal. It was a little over six weeks since the accident. His progress was right on target. *Why did she pull away? Are my scars too repulsive? Did she think I couldn't make love to her, or be a complete man again? Am I pathetic in her eyes?*

Max had become good at driving his truck while wearing the leg braces, but they were coming off in a few weeks anyway. Other than the healing scars, he didn't have lingering signs of his injury except for a slight limp. It could take months of physical therapy before that would go away. He poured a beer and waited for Mario to show up. Nerves set in as he guzzled that beer and cracked open another. Mario was Vic's brother. *Have they talked in depth about us? Does Vic confide in him?* Mario had spent the first week of Max's recovery at Vic's house, but Max had been preoccupied with therapists, and Mario with his business, which he ran over the phone. Max hadn't had the opportunity to see how close Mario and Vic were.

The kitchen window faced the street. Max sat at the table, staring at the almost empty bird feeder in the yard. *I've got to fill that up.* His house was a small Cape Cod, perfect for one person but void of the woman's touch that would make the house a home. He wanted to be loved, and have a family, with Vic. The sound of a car door jarred Max back into the present. Mario, wearing a blue bandanna tied at the nape of his neck and pulled down to his eyebrows, walked up the sidewalk. The long braid swayed from side to side as he walked. He wore Keen sandals and Ray-Ban Aviators. Mario was the hipster and hippie all in one. He wore the look of an over-the-top Telluride ski bum, mixed with an MBA. The crazy part was that he'd lived in New York most of his life.

"Go figure." Max laughed and gave Mario a man hug when he entered the house. "Dude, I've got to get that look." Max teased his new friend about his appearance and the bright-orange Karmann Ghia convertible parked outside.

"Yeah, but you're just too old. I think the cutoff is thirty-five. After that, you have to start looking your age," Mario taunted. "I still have a few years to go."

"Well, if I'm going to run an outdoor-sports-gear store, I need to dress casual. I guess jeans and a T-shirt will do. I'll pass on the hair—that would take years to grow. So, are you ready to see Peekskill?"

"For sure, lead the way, man. I'll drive."

Mario and Max spent an hour and a half between the three vacant stores downtown. Each building had great qualities. The first sat on prime real estate on the corner of two main crossroads. The second had the most square feet of space, and the last was in the best condition. After touring them, they took the listing sheets to a restaurant Max frequented often for lunch. Early-fall weather cooled the air, and the time was right to start gearing up for winter sports. The sidewalk seating gave them the perfect opportunity to people watch. From outside Ruben's Diner, they had a great view of North Division Street and Central Avenue. The table's umbrella shaded the sun, so the streets were crystal clear. Max ordered two microbrews as they assessed the foot traffic. Anywhere on North Division was prime, but Central Avenue seemed a little busier. They were leaning toward the store closest to the intersection of the two streets. Their store would need to be changed to flow with the image of the products they were selling anyway, so they crossed off the one in the best condition. That left the stores with the best location and largest space, but they were on opposite ends of Division Street. Max and Mario decided to take another look at them after lunch.

"So, what have you been up to these last few weeks?" Mario asked through a mouthful of chicken enchilada.

"For now, I'm working three days a week lecturing the kids on wilderness safety and group conduct. It's been fun but nothing like being out there in the middle of it all."

"I hear you, man. I love being outside. It was tough leaving Colorado. Don't get me wrong—I love my home state, but the mountains of Colorado are just eye candy. I'll be honest, Max. I had to make a choice, and I think I made the right one. I wanted to open another store anyway, and what better place than going back to your roots."

Max raised his eyebrows and shook his head in agreement.

"The main reason I left Colorado was because I broke it off with my girlfriend. I caught her cheating with my head ski instructor, my best friend. That really stung, man."

"Damn… that had to be painful." Max looked down and paused, caught up in his own thoughts.

"Max?"

"Yeah?"

"Vic misses you. You should have seen how her eyes lit up when I told her we were meeting today."

Max perked up at the mention of her name. "You saw Vic? How's she doing?"

"She's hanging in there. Dude… you two have something special that can't be denied, so what's the problem?"

"To be honest, I have no idea. I want to make a life with Vic, and I thought we were heading in that direction. The week after you left, she just clammed up. Everything went downhill, and I don't have a clue why. She probably sees me as a cripple, like I've lost my manhood or something. Maybe these scars turn her off. I'm at a loss." Max ordered another round of beer.

"Here's what I know for sure. Women are weird, but we can't live without them. My sister is nuts with a capital N, but she's nuts over you—that's a fact. I wanted her to talk to me about it, but like you said, she clammed up. Somebody has to know what's going on. I bet Mia does."

Chapter Twenty-Nine

Max knew Mia would be the right person to talk to, being Vic's best friend and a great listener. The problem would be getting Mia alone without raising suspicion on Aaron's part. Max didn't want to get between them—that wasn't his intention. He'd have to be careful around Aaron and watch his words if he decided to go that route. Max didn't want to involve other people in his problems.

The lease papers were signed the second week of September. Max and Mario were officially partners in business. They agreed on a two-year lease for the building closest to North Division Street and Central Avenue. The demographics were perfect. There were plenty of passersby in cars and on foot. Peekskill was the right town for opening up an outdoor-sports-gear store. The age group of active adults was just right. This store would thrive with Mario's business smarts and Max's people skills. They wanted the Colorado mountain vibe in downtown Peekskill, starting with the store name. They would name their store Geared Up, and the official opening would be the third weekend of October. Mario arranged to stay with

Vic for six weeks until the store was running smoothly. They had supplies to buy, employees to hire, and a grand opening to promote. Staying in Tarrytown made more sense than going to and from Hunter. It was only twenty-five minutes away, and he didn't want to impose on Max by asking to stay with him.

***

Time moved slowly for Vic. She hadn't seen or spoken to Max in almost a month. She did her best to get out of her funk. Working every day and being with friends saved her. Vic let go of the hope she'd had and moved on. Many evenings were spent with everyone congregating at the Victorian. Sasha hadn't moved in yet, but the house was coming along beautifully. Workers were busy installing the new roof, and the exterior paint job was progressing nicely. The house was emerging with its original dignity and grandeur.

The girls enjoyed paint parties, which always included multiple bottles of Merlot and plenty of smack talk. The dining room walls were slathered with burnt-orange semi-gloss paint. They stretched out blue painter's tape to protect the woodwork even though it was a tedious job. Each person had her specific role and area to work on. Mia teetered on the top step of the ladder, trying to reach the ceiling with the roller. She was tall, athletic, and unanimously assigned to that job. Sasha, being afraid of heights, chose to tape the trim with Tina's help. Karen and Vic painted at eye level while they all chattered at the same time. Background music and wine were constants. An extra case of Merlot sat on the card table at all times. The classic-rock station filled the air as the girls danced around the drop cloth with paintbrushes and rollers in hand.

"Hey, Vic, how's Geared Up coming along?" Sasha asked as she straightened out the blue tape on the door frame. She flicked a piece of tape that was stuck to her ruby-red fingernail. "Mario and Max have to be pretty excited about the progress, right?"

Silence filled the room except for Aerosmith's "Walk This Way" playing in the background. Sasha stopped taping and turned around. Eight eyes stared at her as if she'd just committed a mortal sin. Her transgression would require at least ten Hail Mary's. "Now, what did I do wrong?" She sighed.

"A little empathy would be good," Tina said.

"C'mon, you guys. I got over Jack in five minutes, and we were a real couple."

Mia almost fell off the ladder. "Don't make me come down there and smack you across the face," she yelled from her perch. "Apologize to me, Karen, and Vic... right now!"

"Jeez, you guys... sorry. I was only making conversation."

"Well, converse this." Mia shot the middle finger at Sasha faster than lightning as she shimmied down the ladder. She grabbed Sasha by the nape of the neck. "Outside, now."

"Sorry about Sasha. She doesn't know any better. She

really didn't mean anything by that," Karen said as tears pooled in Vic's eyes.

"I have to let it go. Max and I are over. Nobody needs to tiptoe around me anymore. That's bullshit. You guys have been there for me whenever I needed to talk. I'll be right back." Vic went outside and sat on the porch with Mia and Sasha. Mia was drilling proper etiquette into Sasha's head, harshly.

"Mia... stop, Sasha didn't mean anything by it. She asked a valid question. It's me that needs to get a grip. C'mon, you guys, a group hug... please? Let's take a break and have some wine. Sasha, you asked me a justified question, and I'm going to answer it."

Sasha hung her head and took the walk of shame as she stepped over the threshold and back into the house. "Sorry, everyone, sometimes I just blurt things out. I didn't mean anything by it... really." She gave Tina and Karen a hug and a heartfelt apology.

They sat on the maple floor, side by side in the dining room. The fireplace, which was lit more for ambiance than warmth, glowed with small embers. Mia turned off the music. Sasha filled each empty plastic cup with wine.

Vic started by saying she didn't want any sympathy. If she and Max were meant to be a couple, it would work itself out, somehow, someday. She believed in karma, both good and bad. "Now, to answer your question, Sasha, as far as I know, the store is coming along nicely. Mario said they just hired two college kids for the weekends and a recent graduate to work daily with Max. I've asked Mario about Max's health, and he said Max is doing great. He has a slight limp, but that's all. His leg braces come off in a few days, so that's wonderful news. Mario even said the insurance company gave Max a nice settlement for his Harley, and he already bought another one. I guess he'll start customizing it during the winter months when he isn't helping Mario. It will be slower in Peekskill because of the type of gear they'll sell. The mad rush will be the ski store in Hunter. Max will go there and help out especially on weekends. Any other questions?" she asked with half a smile.

Sasha bounced up and down, raising her hand like a schoolkid. "I do, I do. When are you and Max going to make up?"

Vic groaned with her face in her hands then laughed. "I don't have a clue, honey, but thanks for asking."

***

The Westchester County seat was located in White Plains. Because Mario and Max decided on an LLC, they had to sign documents at the courthouse and register the company trade name before they could officially open for business. Max knew Mario expected to ride together to White Plains since Max would have to pass Tarrytown anyway. He agreed, telling Mario to expect him at ten in the morning. He assumed Vic would be at work.

The 1999 Chevy Silverado lumbered down the highway toward Tarrytown. *Gotta get that exhaust fixed. It's starting to sound like the glass packs on Mia's Camaro.*

Max smiled at the image in his mind. He remembered the day when the paramedics carried Mia to her car after she sprained her ankle. He'd laughed when she pointed to the hotrod black Camaro Z28 sitting in the parking lot. Of course, it had to be her car. Max chuckled as he thought about those crazy few days, months ago. He began to relax as he drove. *Vic will be at work. No worries.* He pulled into the driveway and honked the horn. Mario texted he would be out in a couple of minutes. Max laid his head back against the headrest and closed his eyes. The sun warmed the left side of his face. The open window allowed the breeze to blow gently through the truck. Max's arm was on the window frame, his head propped in his hand. He was dozing off with his head precariously bobbing, ready to hit his chest.

"Hi, Max."

He jumped at Vic's voice, causing her to jump as well. She let out a small giggle.

It's Vic, and she's only inches from my face. "Vic! Why aren't you at work?" Max asked, trying to come to his senses.

"It's Tuesday. Hair Brained is closed. I was out running errands and... you look good. How are you doing?"

"I'm okay, just a small limp with my right leg, but otherwise as good as new. And you?"

The small talk was awkward. Max was sure they both felt it.

"Couldn't be better." Vic smiled but didn't seem

happy. "I'll get Mario for you."

She walked away abruptly and headed for the house. She didn't see Max reaching for her hand.

Mario came out and got into the passenger side of the truck. "Okay, man—let's make this business official," not commenting on the brief encounter with Vic.

***

Vic peered out between the slats of the blinds as they drove away. Tears streamed down her cheeks and gathered at her chin before falling to her pink T-shirt.

***

Ten days remained before the grand opening. Karen had volunteered her services for the promotion, but as soon as Max and Mario realized what an asset she was, they hired her full-time. She would be the PR representative for both stores. Karen was good at what she did but had an agenda all her own. She wanted to get closer to Mario. If it had to start out as business only, so be it. It was a start. Timing was everything, and Karen would remain patient.

She took charge of all the promotional planning. She ran the ads, printed the flyers and brochures, and hired teenagers to walk the streets of Peekskill handing them out. She ran the idea past Mario and Max of a 10 percent discount on all purchases on the day of the grand opening. She also suggested a grand prize of two hundred Geared Up Bucks for in-store merchandise to the thousandth person coming through the doors on their opening

221

weekend. She sent out invitations to everyone they knew to attend the grand opening. There would be an after-party for their closest friends—Karen reserved the beautiful Stonewater Grille's canopied terrace deck for Friday night, October 17.

"That should get the town buzzing," she said as they ended the day at Ruben's. The three sat at an outdoor table on the sidewalk, each with a cold pint in hand. Geared Up was directly across the street. Trying to take on the role of an unbiased customer, each gave an opinion of the store from the restaurant side, looking toward it. Max liked the facade but suggested potted evergreens on either side of the entrance to give it an outdoor feel.

"Great idea—I like it," Karen said.

"I do too. I'd also put a bicycle rack, some hooks for dog leashes, and dog water bowls outside," Mario added. "That's the type of extras people like. The stores in Colorado do it. I'm already doing it in Hunter. What do you think, Karen?"

"I like everything you both said. The only additional thing I'd do is make the name of the store larger on the windows. We have windows facing both major streets. We need the name on each side in bold letters. Also, I really like the idea of a cool awning over the door. It will look classy and inviting but not over the top. I can take care of all of that if you two agree."

"Sounds good to me. Mario?"

Mario looked at Karen and smiled. "I say yes. Plus the smartest move we've made so far is bringing Karen on board. You're exactly what we need."

And you're exactly what I need, she thought, giving him her sultriest smile in return.

Chapter Thirty

The seasons were changing. Summer heat and humidity waned into crisp fall mornings. Skies darkened earlier, and night set in by seven in the evening.

Mario brought home Vic's invitation for the grand opening and after-party. He handed it to her as she sat on the couch, watching sit-com reruns and eating Doritos.

"Now what?" Vic paused the TV and tore open the envelope. She reached for her bubblegum-pink readers, which were lying on the coffee table.

Mario planted himself in front of her, standing his ground. With his arms crossed, he waited for her protests. She wouldn't get off easy.

The pleading began. "Mario…" She dropped back on the couch, pouting like a child and burrowing under the pillows.

"Really, Vic, how old are you—five? I'm your brother, and you're going to attend this grand opening and party to make *me* happy. What a novel idea, something that isn't about you."

"You don't have to be so nasty to me," she whined.

"I do if it's the only way to get your attention. Saturday morning, we're going shopping together."

"What the hell for?" she grumbled, throwing the remote at him.

"I need a great looking suit for the after-party, and you, my crazy Puerto Rican sister? You're going to buy a smokin' hot dress that will make Max weak in the knees when he sees you. We'll call it the cost of doing business. Come hell or high water, I'm going to rally the troops and get you two lovebirds back together. I don't need a brain-dead business partner or a brain-dead sister on my hands. I planned to let it go, but you're better together than apart, so that's how it's going to be. Any questions?"

"Yeah... who made you my boss?" Vic threw a couch pillow at him and laughed. "I love you, Bro, even though you're neurotic and a pain in my oversized ass."

"So, we have a deal for Saturday morning? I'll even buy the dress for you," he said, kissing her forehead.

"Yeah... whatever, you have a deal."

***

Mario and Vic took the train into the city Saturday morning. They decided to make it a fun day of shopping, sightseeing, and eating. No visiting crazy cousins, just the two siblings enjoying each other's company. Before shopping began, they toured The Cloisters in Upper Manhattan. Vic remembered the family doing outings together a few times a year when she was young. Money was tight, so they would decide as a group where to go.

They enjoyed The Cloisters, even as children, and chose that most often. They loved to see the peaceful gardens and magnificent collections. It was hard for Vic to remember, but she knew the visits had stopped abruptly for some reason.

She sat alone on the only granite bench in the shade of that large cypress tree. The far end of the gardens didn't get many visitors. It was a quiet and forgotten place. Small stones filled her hand. She studied them closely like prized possessions. She twisted each one between her fingers until the light hit it just right. Some held tiny grains of quartz that glistened when she found a ray of sun. Vic smiled at them. Her pleasure in these stones was almost childlike. Memories from her youth ran through her mind—some vivid, some faint. She remembered sitting on that very bench long ago, holding rocks and being mesmerized by their sparkling colors. She couldn't have been more than six. She was hidden within the shade of the large cypress tree. She fell asleep, and her family couldn't find her. Later, she learned that they'd called her name over and over again. They frantically searched for hours and even involved security. Her oldest brother, Carlos, eventually found her and called her horrible names for upsetting everyone. They missed lunch and most of the exhibits because of her. It was all her fault. She was stupid and ugly with that long, frizzy hair. She'd ruined their day. Her siblings were mad at her for weeks. They never returned to The Cloisters. Even her parents said it was because she'd traumatized everyone. The memories were sketchy at best, but she was sure they were true. *Could that have something to do with my insecurities?*

"Sis? I knew I'd find you here." Mario approached her. He'd been too young to remember that day but was told about it from his brothers every time Vic did something wrong.

"Mario, do you think Carlos and the others have something against me? We aren't close like you and I are."

"We're the youngest—of course we'd be closer. How about lunch? Have you seen enough?" Mario didn't want Vic to bring up bad memories. Today needed to be a day filled with fun and laughter.

They left The Cloisters, and the memories, behind. The ten-minute walk through Fort Tryon Park was relaxing. They caught up on some much-needed bonding, brother-and-sister style. The forty-five minute subway ride to midtown offered great people watching. Vic and Mario took turns jabbing each other in the side when someone interesting caught their attention. They took in the sights and the jarring of the train as it made its starts and stops while getting closer to midtown and the shopping district.

"Would you ever trade small-town life for this craziness, Mario?"

"Never in a hundred lifetimes. How about you?"

"Nope—my feet are planted in Tarrytown for good."

They walked for several hours, enjoying everything Times Square had to offer. Lights flashing, cabs honking, and people hurrying to get somewhere—often with scowls on their faces while they pushed through the crowds—

mesmerized Vic and Mario. They ducked into a Starbucks for an espresso. A boost of energy would hold them over. They fell into the cushy chairs, both exhaling at the same time. Vic brought the demitasse close to her nose and inhaled the deep-brown elixir. The strong coffee smelled heavenly. It was the magic potion that would get them through shopping. Their legs were tired, and they still had hours to go.

"Okay, Sis, where do you want to shop?" Mario asked, hoping she would pick a store nearby.

"Let's go to Macy's. We can both find what we need there. To be honest, I'm exhausted already. Maybe we should have lunch first to perk us up."

She did an Internet search and found a pizzeria, halfway to Macy's, with good reviews and four stars. "We only have a few blocks to walk on Seventh Avenue. C'mon, we're out of here."

The pizzeria was small. Vic and Mario needed to adjust their eyes before they could see the dimly lit room. Six booths lined the wall. A table with four chairs sat on either side of the door. Red-checked tablecloths and an Italian motif decorated the tiny establishment. The smell of pizza baking in the stone oven was divine. A portly Italian man threw dough to the delight of several families in the booths. It was a show all its own.

Mario and Vic dropped into the seats of the train back to Tarrytown at six o'clock. Vic was certain her arms were longer just from the weight of the bags they'd carried around for hours.

"Was that an awesome day or what?" Mario asked, his voice sounding exhausted.

"Yeah, and you know what?"

"What?" Mario raised his eyebrows and turned his head toward her.

"We're going to be the hottest-looking siblings at that party."

"I'm sure we'll be the only siblings at that party."

"Yeah, but we're still going to be the hottest."

They both dozed off, clutching their bags.

***

Vic gathered the girls for lunch at her house on Tuesday. Finger food, sandwiches, and sweets filled the table. Chilled sangria was in the beautiful, cut-glass pitcher she'd inherited from her grandmother. Slices of strawberries, oranges, and limes bobbed up and down with each pour. A variety of cheese cubes with colorful toothpicks was served on Fiestaware, in the flamingo shade.

"This is different, Vic. We always meet somewhere for lunch. What gives?" Karen asked, after air kisses had been exchanged.

"Nothing much, I just wanted my besties here for lunch. I'm going to model the dress Mario bought me Saturday when we went to the city."

"Oh, cool," Sasha said, bouncing in her chair. "Everyone is going to the grand opening Friday night, right?" She looked around, acknowledging everyone's affirmative nods.

"I'll admit I'm kind of nervous." Vic wiped imaginary crumbs off the tablecloth as she spoke.

"We'll have a great time. You should be proud of Mario. This is… what, his third store now?" Mia already knew the answer but was trying to get Vic's mind off of Max. She popped a handful of green olives into her mouth. "So, go put on the dress. We're dying to see it."

"Okay, but it's kind of racy, and I want you guys to know it was Mario who picked it out—even though I probably would have picked out the same dress. I'm just saying." Vic giggled and trotted off to the bedroom.

"Friday night should be interesting," Tina said.

They heard the clip-clop of heels coming toward them from the hallway. Vic stopped before turning the corner to build the suspense. There were four waiting bodies at the kitchen table with eyes bulging and mouths agape.

"Okay… here I come." She was giggling again.

"Well do it already, for crap's sake," they said in unison.

"Holy mother of Jesus and God—you look better than me!" Sasha blurted out.

Everyone rolled their eyes and laughed at the nonsense that always spewed from Sasha's mouth. A grin spread across Vic's face as she pranced around like a new filly full of energy and life. The silver, shimmery dress clung to her every curve. Thin spaghetti straps were all that dangerously held up her ample breasts, and they still heaved over the décolletage. The hemline was so short it barely covered the Kardashian-sized butt Vic loved or hated, depending on what she was wearing at the time.

"Oh my friggin' God—how are you going to sit in that thing?" Mia asked, her mouth still gaping open, her green olives not fully swallowed.

"I have no idea. I guess I'll stand all night. I'm not putting it on until we get to the after-party anyway. At the grand opening, I'll be casual like everyone else." Vic was still giggling. "Can you believe Mario picked this out?"

"Um… duh… he's a guy," Tina said.

"I've got a great idea," Karen added. "Let's all change into hot-as-hell, provocative dresses once we get to the after-party. That way, Vic won't look like a slut all by herself. We can join her. It will be a riot!"

"Damn girl—you're hanging out with Sasha too much," Mia said, cracking up. "But, I'll admit, it is a great idea. Let's do it. None of our guys will be able to take their eyes off of us."

"That's hilarious, Mia, since you're the only one with a guy," Vic said.

"True, but by the end of the night, who knows?"

Chapter Thirty-One

Friday arrived, and the grand opening was in full swing. People lined up to take advantage of the ten percent discount on their merchandise. Everyone hoped to be the winner of the two hundred dollars in Geared Up Bucks.

Karen made sure everything ran smoothly, like a well-oiled machine. *No hiccups, no mistakes. Today has to be perfect.* Mario was well aware of her business sense and abilities, but she also wanted him to notice her as a single woman interested in him.

A local catering service had snacks and beverages set up along the street in front of the store entrance. Dog owners were given biscuits for their beloved pets. Water bowls were filled with fresh water every half hour for those thirsty pooches. Free face painting and small toys were given to the kids. Helium balloons tied to the potted evergreens swayed in the breeze. Even the local TV station and *Daily Gazette* stopped by to take pictures and get a quick interview with either Max or Mario. Mia ran around, snapping candid shots and videos for their own memories.

Everyone pitched in to get the store off to a great start. Vic and Max bumped into each other constantly—she, stocking shelves and he, helping customers. They politely apologized each and every time. Sideways glances and smiles lit the girls' faces as they deliberately found ways to push Vic and Max together.

The first day wound down, and the crowd had dispersed by five thirty. At six o'clock, the store closed with everyone sighing from exhaustion. The grand opening was a huge success with total sales of $6,239.00 for the day. It was cause for celebration.

The after-party would begin at seven thirty. The trunk of Karen's car was filled with gorgeous dresses sheathed in garment bags. Shoe boxes and handbags sat on the floor in the backseat. The girls left first for the Inn along the Hudson to change clothes and freshen up. They'd rented one room for the night just to have a place to shower and change. Aaron, Max, and Mario stayed behind to restock, straighten up, and close the store.

The suite they'd reserved was crowded with women. Glamorous dresses lay across the beds. Shoes were tripped over, and nonstop chatter filled the room. They took turns speed showering and applying makeup in the brightly lit bathroom. The large dresser with a full-sized mirror was their staging area for hair and primping. By seven fifteen, the girls were transformed into Cinderella's on their way to the ball. Mia took individual pictures of each of them as well as a group shot, using the timer and tripod. They were indeed like sisters. Each had her own distinct beauty and quirky personality, but they all had the same amount of love in their hearts with a little extra waiting to be appreciated by a good man.

"My God, if the way we look doesn't stop some living, breathing man in his tracks tonight, we don't have a damn prayer," Tina said.

They each gave a nod of approval to the others and headed toward the elevator.

A sandwich board by the outer doors of the Stonewater Grille congratulated Geared Up for opening its new store in town. A message on the board said the Grille was closed to the public that night, but the owners of Geared Up welcomed invited guests to their private after-party being held on the canopied terrace. Mia snapped a few shots of the sandwich board to add to her photo collection. A memory album would be assembled for Mario and Max, compliments of Mia James, photographer extraordinaire. The five beauties stood in front of the double doors that led to the party. They could hear guests reveling on the other side. By the sound of it, there was quite a crowd.

"Are you lovelies ready to go in?" Sasha asked, looking stunning herself.

They gave each other the once-over, checking for lipstick on their teeth, toilet paper on their heels, or any possible clothing malfunction. They were good to go. Sasha pulled one door open, nodded to Mia, and she opened the other. They entered, strutting in as though they owned the place, and by the expression on everyone's faces, they did. Whispers, gasps, and wolf whistles echoed throughout the restaurant and terrace. Max and Aaron were spellbound while Mario cupped his hands around his mouth and yelped like a coyote between shouts of approval. A slow applause erupted into loud cheers. Heads bobbing up and down, in nods of "uh-huh-oh-yeah," told the girls they were a unanimous hit with the crowd, especially the men.

Mia watched Vic out of the corner of her eye. Her friend was staring at Max with a targeted laser-beam gaze. Max himself stood frozen in place with his mouth wide open. He definitely needed assistance peeling his eyes off of her. Mia was certain she saw a string of drool drop to the lapel of his sports jacket. Aaron wasn't much better. The stupid, half-cocked smile plastered across his face made Mia burst out laughing. The two men needed to be leashed that night. Mia knew Aaron would be on her like a fly on shit. Even Mario perked up and seemed to be watching Karen as if he'd just had an epiphany. He may as well have slapped himself across the head and said, "I could have had a V8."

Hours passed, and the party hummed along perfectly. Guests mingled and offered congratulatory handshakes and pats on the back. The scent of cigars wafted through the air from the terrace. Waiters whisked by with trays of Champagne and assorted hors d'oeuvres.

"Hey, babe, you wanna get lucky later?" Aaron whispered in Mia's ear. He wrapped his arms around her and kissed her neck. "I've never seen anyone as beautiful as you in my life, Mia. That's for damn sure. You take my breath away."

"I love you so much. And hell yeah, I want to get lucky later," she said, laughing. "I know one thing for sure."

"What's that?"

"I'm already lucky. I have to pinch myself every day to make sure I'm not dreaming." Mia nudged Aaron when she saw Vic walk down the hallway and enter the ladies' room. Max followed her, lingering in the area, waiting for her to exit. "I wonder how this is going to play out."

***

"Oh, for the love of crap, how am I going to go to the bathroom?"

"Excuse me?" A meek voice from the next stall startled Vic.

"Shit... I'm sorry, I didn't realize anyone else was in here. It's just that my dress is so friggin' tight. I'll manage." *Okay, so I'll have to squirm and twist until I have my dress up to my waist, and then my Spanx will have to go down to my knees. Maybe then I can sit, for crap's sake. If my damn ass wasn't so big...*

***

Max paced the hallway. His hands were jammed deep in the pockets of the perfect-fitting pants he wore. His forehead was tight with anxiety. *What the hell is she doing in there for so long?* The door swung open. It was the other woman. Max smiled and moved down the hall a bit. He didn't want to look like a ladies' room stalker. Five more minutes he paced, hoping he didn't seem overly conspicuous. Finally, the door opened again. Vic came out, grumbling and cursing under her breath about the damn dress. She pulled and twisted at the seams as she walked. Vic didn't look up until it was too late, and she plowed right into Max. He was stunned. She was humiliated. They both turned a deep crimson red.

"Oh, for Pete's sake, I'm so sorry, Max. I should watch where the hell I'm going. It's just this stupid…"

He gently put his fingers over her ruby-red lips. "Shhh… Vic… you're a vision of beauty, like a goddess. I can't take my eyes off of you, and I really don't want to, either. I've never felt like this before. My heart is pounding through my chest right now." He took her hand and pressed it against his chest. "Can you feel how hard it's beating?"

"Yes."

"I can't keep up this facade any longer, Vic. I need you in my life. We have to come to terms with this. Can we go somewhere and talk?"

"Tonight isn't the right time or place, Max. This is a celebration party. It's about the store's grand opening, not us."

"How about tomorrow? I'll come to Tarrytown after we close. Let me buy you dinner. Please say yes."

She stared a hole in the floor then said, "Okay. Call me when you're on your way. I'll meet you at Morey's."

Time stood still as neither knew what to say next. Max spoke first. "Okay, then… I guess we'll talk tomorrow night. Vic?"

She looked up with a glimmer of hope in her eyes.

"You're the most beautiful woman I've ever seen." He smiled and went back to the party.

Chapter Thirty-Two

The party ended at one in the morning, and everybody was exhausted but exhilarated. It had been quite a day. A few stragglers lingered. The building was about to close, but Aaron, Mia, Max, Mario, and Vic remained. They sat at a table with wine stains covering the cloth and drank coffee before they went their separate ways. They laughed about the evening, especially the moment when the girls walked in and all jaws dropped.

"I'll admit, that was a classic move for the five of you. We should have expected it," Aaron joked.

"Yeah, Aaron, you should have seen the expression on your face. Damn…" Vic snickered and gave a sideways glance at Max. "And you, Max—your mouth hung open for at least thirty seconds."

They roared with laughter at the men's expense.

Vic scanned the room, pretending to gaze beyond Max. She noticed the corners of his mouth turning up. He smiled, knowing full well what she was doing. He gave her a wink. Relief swept through her. *Good… I didn't overdo it.*

"I guess it's time to head home. It's been a long first

day," Mario said. "Sis, are you ready?"

"Sure, Bro, I'll catch up with you in a minute." Vic said good night to Aaron and Mia, and walked out to the terrace. She breathed in the scent of the nearby Hudson River. Crickets chirped, and the echoes of frogs lingered in the crisp night air. Vic needed a few minutes to clear her head. There might be a chance with Max after all, but her truth had to be told first. Max deserved that. Deep insecurities about Max and Mia haunted her. The guilt about his accident weighed heavily on her. *He must have been wondering why I treated him so indifferently that night as he drove down the dark highway on his motorcycle. If only I hadn't pushed him away…*

"Vic? What are you doing out here alone?"

She jumped at the sound of his voice. Deep in her own misery and guilt, Vic didn't hear Max come up behind her. "Max, you scared me. I had no idea you were standing there. I'm leaving now. I just needed some fresh air."

He came closer until they were only inches apart. His breath warmed her skin. The scent of Montblanc Legend filled her nostrils, causing her heart to skip a beat, or two. Vic's knees wobbled, ready to buckle at any second.

"Mario is waiting for me. I should go." *I can't do this until I come clean with you, Max.*

He backed away and leaned against the railing, his arms crossed in frustration. "Okay, if you say so. I'll see you tomorrow night at Morey's, right?"

"Yes, at Morey's. Good night."

"Good night, Vic."

***

The drive back to Tarrytown wasn't long. Aaron took his time because of the late hour and the dark road. "Did you have fun tonight, honey?"

"Yeah, it was great. I'm so happy for Max and Mario. The store is going to be a huge success. You're staying over tonight, aren't you?"

"Sure, babe. What do you think about living together? Full-time, I mean. Are you ready for that—to give up your house and live with me?" Aaron reached over the console and squeezed Mia's hand. "Our dreams are coming true, honey. All that's left is marriage and a family." He glanced at her and smiled.

Those dimples and perfect white teeth had stolen her heart months ago, but now Mia was overwhelmed with joy at the thought of marrying Aaron. "I'll live with you in sin for a while, Aaron, but you better make an honest woman out of me before too long. I don't want to be the talk of the town. I have a reputation to uphold, mister."

"So, that's a yes?"

"Of course, it's a yes. I love you. Now get me home so you can ravish me like you promised."

"Yes ma'am."

***

Max watched the clock all day even though the store kept him busy. He had new employees to work with and customers to help. The thought of actually spending time with Vic later had him nervous. He wasn't sure how it would go, but he was certain tonight's conversation would tell him if they had a chance to start over or not. Max rang up purchases and stocked the shelves. Boxes of T-shirts needed to be opened, and prices had to be set. Mario sat in the back room, going through the wholesale catalog. They needed snowshoes, cross-country skis, and cold-weather camping gear. Max straightened out the tent display and lined up the sleeping bags along the wall. He checked the mountain bikes outside on the rack to make sure they all had price tags.

"Hey, Max, you wanna grab some lunch? My stomach is growling, dude."

"Sure. Buckley's is pretty good. It's just down the street. I'll tell the kids we're leaving."

Max and Mario were getting close. They shared the same work ethic and outlook on life: work hard, play harder. But at thirty-seven, Max wanted more. He wanted Vic.

"Mario, do you mind if I speak candidly?"

"You mean about Vic?"

"Is it that obvious?" Max rubbed the furrows in his forehead. "Damn… it's hard to get a read on her. We're meeting later, and I don't have a clue what to expect."

"Here's what I can tell you for sure. Vic's crazy about you—that much I know. She's thirty-three years old, and I'm sure that messed-up biological clock ticking in her head is throwing alarms off every day. She had it rough growing up, being the only girl with three brothers. We gave her a lot of shit, and I think she still carries some of those scars. It's hard to believe, as beautiful as Vic is, that she has one ounce of insecurity, but she does. She puts on the hard facade to cover it up. Go easy on her, Max. Vic loves you, and I'm certain that love is mutual. You guys can work it out. I wouldn't mind having my business partner as part of our family someday. Take it slow, and give her a little slack. She'll come around. Now, enough about Vic, let's have lunch."

Max felt better after talking to Mario. Who would know better than Vic's own brother? There was hope, and for now, his nerves had settled down.

They finished with another great day. The customers loved the store and the outdoor, wilderness theme they'd given it. Thanks to Max, during the remodeling they'd installed plank floors and had the walls painted with a woodsy mural. Old beams ran across the length of the ceiling, purchased from a retired farmer who'd had his barn dismantled. The shelves were heaving with high-tech outdoor gear and cold-weather clothing in preparation for winter. They carried regular and long-sleeved T-shirts, all of them 100 percent organic cotton. The store was perfect for Peekskill—they'd hit a home run with the demographics. Max and Mario were in it for the long haul.

"See you tomorrow, bro," Mario said to Max with a man hug. He locked the outer door and set the alarm. "Good luck with Vic. I really mean that, man."

"Thanks for the insight earlier. I'll talk to you tomorrow." Max drove the seven blocks to his house to shower and change clothes. He wanted to look good for Vic. He imagined their future together as he drove. They would live in Tarrytown because Vic loved it there. It was a great town, and other than the store, Peekskill didn't hold any special significance for Max. Three kids sounded nice—two boys and a girl. Max laughed out loud, picturing how Vic would style their little girl's hair. *Poor thing! The kids would have the best mommy in the world though. She's fierce with her love.*

He went in the house to get ready, full of optimism. Max dressed in black jeans, a royal-blue, long-sleeved V-neck tee, and a black leather coat. He combed back his hair and shook his head, letting the hair fall naturally, waves forming as it dried. The scent of Montblanc Legend filled the bathroom as he spritzed it on his hands, rubbed them together, and patted areas of his neck and arms. Max checked his reflection in the hall mirror, flipped on the porch light, and locked the door behind him. He climbed into his truck and left for Tarrytown. He called Vic to say he was on his way. He would meet her at Morey's at seven in the evening.

***

Vic couldn't do a thing with her hair. "Damn it. Of all nights to look like a piece of shit! That's it—this mess is going in a knot on top of my head." Vic leaned over, twisted the damp hair into a long rope, and wound it around her hand until it resembled a black cinnamon roll. The bun was secured to the top of her head with two pieces of a chopstick snapped in half. "Ugh… I swear I'm getting a migraine from nerves. I'll probably start my period, too, with the luck I have." She downed four Ibuprofen for good measure and tore open her closet, throwing outfits on the bed. "Not this… or that. The green dress makes me look fat, and these pants accentuate my huge ass. Oh, for crap's sake, I need a friggin' muumuu." After fifteen minutes of groaning and swearing, Vic decided on a pair of stretchy pink leggings with a black, sheer top cinched at the waist with a wide patent-leather belt. Pink chandelier Swarovski crystal earrings dangled from her earlobes. Her makeup and fingernails were perfect. A dab of Chanel behind her ears and wrists, and she was ready to go. "Oh… what the hell." She dabbed even more perfume between her breasts.

The grandfather clock chimed every fifteen minutes. She heard it from the bedroom. *It must be quarter to seven. I'm out of here.*

The five-minute drive to Morey's didn't give Vic enough time to get nervous. It took longer to find a parking spot and walk inside. She looked around and saw the flash of an arm waving at her. Max stood up and grinned at her from the farthest table, in the corner of the dining room.

Why the hell is Morey's so jammed tonight? Then she remembered it was Saturday. *Duh… I'm not accustomed to being in here on weekends.* "Hi, Max. Sorry about the crowd. I forgot how crazy this place gets on Saturday nights."

"Do you have any other suggestions, maybe someplace a little quieter? By the way, you look beautiful. I like that hairstyle. It's different."

They both burst out laughing when she punched him in the arm.

"C'mon—follow me," she said.

They walked out into the cool night. The full moon illuminated the sky, accented by a million twinkling stars.

"How far are we going, Vic? You're shaking already." He apprehensively put his arm around her to warm her up. She didn't resist.

"Not far. Just over to Amelia's. It's quieter there—no TVs or rowdy people."

They stepped over the threshold into the warm restaurant. It instantly felt good. Vic's shoulders relaxed. There were only ten other people inside. "This is better. We'll be able to talk and actually hear each other."

They sat at a booth in the back corner. The tables near them were empty, and they were a good distance from the bar and kitchen. Amelia's was open until ten nightly, but most of their customers were lunchtime people from the neighboring businesses downtown. The weekend party crowd usually went to Bottoms Up or Morey's. This was just right.

Chapter Thirty-Three

Carmen, one of the longtime waitresses, brought menus to their darkened, quiet booth. "Hey, Vic, what's up, girl? Who's this hunka-hunka burning love? I don't think I've had the pleasure."

Max laughed while a red blush colored his cheeks. His sideways glance and eye roll toward Vic got them all laughing.

"Seriously, Carmen, you are a woman out of control. This is my friend, Max. Max, this is crazy Carmen. We've known each other since junior high."

"Nice to meet you, Max. I hope Vic is taking good care of you." She gave him a slow and deliberate once-over, followed by a wink. "What can I get you to drink, honey?"

"I'll have an Abbey Ale, please."

"You got it, doll. I'll get you a glass of Merlot, Vic. I'll be back in a minute."

"So, this is what living in Tarrytown would be like, huh? Everyone knows each other, whether you want them to, or not. It's kind of charming. I could get used to it."

Vic began to fumble. Max was making innuendos. She

had to change the subject. It was far too early to be serious. It would take at least two glasses of wine before she'd be able to muster up the courage to say what she needed to. Vic grabbed a menu and tried to look interested in the dinner choices. "Do you know what you want, Max?"

A serious expression came over his face. "Yes, Vic, I know exactly what I want. My question is, do you want the same thing?"

She looked up from the menu, held his gaze, and then realized he wasn't talking about dinner. Vic stammered, not sure of the response to give. Right then, she could only speak in gibberish. She fidgeted with the napkin on her lap and fussed with her hair.

"Vic?"

"I'm trying to think of the words. Honesty is the best policy, right? I was taught that in catechism."

Max laughed out loud again. "Honey, I don't think you learned that in catechism, but I agree, honesty is the best policy. Tell me what's going on in that beautiful head of yours."

"It's hard for me to talk about. I'm afraid to say the words."

"Say whatever is on your mind. We'll sort it out together."

"Okay... I'm just going to blurt it out. Mia told me about the two of you. The sex, I mean. I'm insecure because she's so beautiful, and you had an instant connection."

Max took a large gulp of his beer and paused. An expression Vic didn't recognize took over his entire face. He clearly hadn't seen that coming, and he looked stunned. Vic stared at him, wondering if the redness in his face was from anger or embarrassment.

"Say something... please."

He cleared his throat and took another gulp of beer. "I agree with everything you said. Mia is really beautiful, and we did have an instant connection. We were also kind of thrown together by accident. What happened wasn't planned... well... except the second time. Shit... this is hard to talk about. Can you take everything I'm going to say?"

"I hope so."

"I've been a lost soul for a long time. That's a whole different story, and I don't want to drift off this subject right now. Everything happened when Mia sprained her ankle, but apparently you know that. We were stuck together overnight and did a lot of talking. Mia confided in me, saying how her husband was cheating on her. She had a need right then, and obviously, I did too. I don't know how long Mia went without intimacy, but me? It was years. It just happened, Vic. Neither of us have regrets, but that doesn't mean we haven't moved on. Sex is a beautiful thing, sweetheart, and nothing to be ashamed of, given the right circumstances. Mia and I had a talk the day I met you. She told me she was in love with someone else. I respect her honesty, then and now. The last thing I would ever do is mess up her life when she just got it back on track. Aaron seems like a great guy, and they're happy together. Now, as far as beautiful, when was the last time you looked in the mirror?"

"Less than an hour ago," she said with the tiniest smile.

Max grinned. "I didn't mean it literally. You're drop-dead gorgeous, Vic. My God, woman, do you have any idea how my heart flutters when I see you? My pulse beats twice as fast as normal, and I get butterflies in my stomach. Yeah... that doesn't sound very manly. What I'm trying to say is, I want a real relationship, and I want it with you. I want us to be together by choice, not by need or accident. You don't have to worry about Mia and me, ever."

A tear slid down Vic's cheek and she looked away, trying not to appear vulnerable. "My ass is too big, and I have screwed-up hair."

"Vic, look at me... please." Max came around to her side of the booth and sat next to her. She turned toward him, and he gently wiped her wet cheek with his fingertip.

"You're perfect, absolutely perfect. Honey, you don't always have to be so tough. Soft is good, too." He smiled and kissed her eyelids.

"Max, there's something else I need to tell you before I can be at peace."

He looked at her quizzically. "There's more?"

"Yes. It's about the party at my house for Mia and Aaron, and the way I treated you. There's no excuse for my behavior that night. Those damn insecurities took over my mind, and jealousy filled my heart. You wouldn't have left when you did if I wasn't behaving that way. You might have spent the night—who knows? Your accident was my fault. You were distracted, weren't you? You hit the deer because your mind was on the way I treated you. I know it's true. You're such a careful driver. I don't know if I can get over the guilt in my heart."

"None of it was your fault," he said. "I wasn't thinking about us—I was just enjoying the ride. The fresh evening air and the peaceful country highway felt magical. I was one with the road on my bike until my pant leg got stuck in the foot peg. I reached down to pull it out, and the bike wobbled a little. I overcorrected and hit the deer. Vic, it wasn't even on the road. It was standing on the side of the ditch. I hit it because of my own stupidity. Don't blame yourself. I made the mistake, not you. It was an accident, honey, nothing more. When I left your house that night, I did wonder why you seemed off, but I chalked it up to anxiety. Putting a big party together takes work. Isn't that why you were short with me?"

"No. It was because I saw you and Mia together in the driveway. I saw you hug and heard you say you loved each other."

"You have no idea what that was about." Max fidgeted and rearranged himself in the booth.

"Yes, I do. Mia told me. That's why I feel so terrible. I misunderstood your actions and let my fears get the best of me. I didn't trust you that night, or Mia, my best friend in the entire world. I had to come clean about all my fears and insecurities tonight, or I would never be able to go forward with you. The burden and guilt inside was eating away at me. I need your forgiveness, Max. I love you, and I don't want secrets between us."

"Honey, if at any time something seems off to you, don't sit on it and let it stew. Just come out and say what's on your mind. Now... back to what you just said. You love me?" Max broke into a huge, dimpled grin. He took her face in his hands and kissed her tear-stained cheeks.

***

He would never tell her the truth—he couldn't. The lie that passed his lips about hitting the deer had to stay with him, and only him, forever. Vic would never let go of her guilt if Max really told her how the accident had happened. "Distracted" was putting it lightly. Max had hit the deer because of his distraction... over her. He couldn't focus on the road ahead because his mind was too full of doubts about Vic. There never was an issue with the foot peg, but he loved Vic. He had to tell her the lie for her own peace of mind. She had to forgive herself if she ever wanted to get over her insecurities.

"So, you didn't hit the deer because of me? And you love everything about me, even the frizzy bun on my head, and my big ass? You don't think Mia is more beautiful with her gorgeous smooth blond hair?"

"Um... let's see if I have this in the right order. Nope... yep... and another nope. C'mon sweetheart—let's get out of here."

They left Amelia's. Max held her close as they walked.

They stopped at the gazebo in the town square. Streetlights in the distance gently illuminated the white Victorian structure. Faint music and laughter echoed from the sports bars a few blocks away. Max faced Vic and reached around her head. He gently removed the chopsticks from her hair, letting the still-damp raven locks tumble to the center of her back. He inhaled the fresh scent of honeysuckle shampoo as he buried his face in her black mane and nuzzled her softly. His lips were warm against her skin. Max kissed her eyes, her nose, and her neck. Their mouths met—barely at first. The passion escalated as their anxiety faded.

"I love you, Vic. Don't ever doubt that. You're the woman I want—nobody else." He kissed her so passionately it took her breath away. There was love and fire between them. It couldn't be denied. Vic and Max were meant to be together. He took her butt in his hands and gave each cheek a squeeze. "Victoria Maria Alonso, I wouldn't trade this for anything in the world. You're my love and my life… forever."

THE END

Book three in *Like Sisters* series is available now at:

http://briamarche.com/books/

Be the first to be notified of new releases at:

http://briamarche.com/newsletter/

Visit my website at:

http://briamarche.com/

ACKNOWLEDGMENTS

My love, thanks, and deep appreciation go out to all of the people who have supported me from my initial dream of becoming a writer to reading the words "THE END" when I finished my very first novel. There were no scoffs, laughs or negativity. Family and friends continue to help me with constructive criticism, high fives, cheers, and words of encouragement. From my editor and cover designer to my formatter in a faraway country, you have made my journey so much easier. Erik, I appreciate you more than you could imagine. You have been there for me since before I wrote the very first word. Rochelle, you're the best promoter I could ask for. Photographer Karen Nelson made the "About the Author" photo of me look great. Plus she is an avid supporter and my fun-loving sister.

16163678R00154

Printed in Great Britain
by Amazon